WOUNDED
HEARTS/
HEALED
SOULS

WOUNDED HEARTS/ HEALED SOULS

Miss CC

XULON PRESS

Xulon Press
2301 Lucien Way #415
Maitland, FL 32751
407.339.4217
www.xulonpress.com

Paperback ISBN-13: 978-1-66286-685-2
Ebook ISBN-13: 978-1-66286-686-9

PREQUEL

The summer sun blazed in the sky and the men were working on the logs from the trees they cut down. The logs were split, and the smaller branches cut off so they would roll down smoother to the Nisqually river to be transported to the mill owned by James Smith. Patrick O'Donnell was supervising the operation when his foreman ran up to him and said that a tree fell the wrong way and landed on top of one of the loggers. Patrick ran down the hill toward the fallen tree. When he got there the logger had been rescued and was being cared for by the other loggers. Fortunately, he only had a broken leg. Two of the men, Danny, one of the O'Donnell brothers, and Bucky Schulz were getting the injured logger on the wagon when Patrick came over to them.

"Sam, I hope you get better soon," Patrick said with a worried look on his face.

"Danny, you, and Bucky get him to town, I think he will have to rest up at Josie's until we can get a doctor in town. But hurry back, we have a deadline to meet, and these logs need to be finished by today!" Patrick walked off to check on another section they had been logging. Danny jumped in the front and took the reins, and Bucky got in the back next to Sam. The road was rough as they left, but they only had about 5 miles to go.

Meanwhile, Patrick was back at his 'office' when Mr. Smith stopped in.

"Patrick, may I have a word with you?" Mr. Smith asked.

"Yes of course James, what is it?"

"I just saw Danny driving away with Sam and Bucky, you lost another hand! How are you going to get my order done? I have a deadline you know!"

Patrick finished what he was doing and as he looked up from his desk, he saw Aiden walking in. Aiden had come to talk to Patrick but saw James was there, so he began to turn around to leave, then Patrick said, "No, stay Aiden! I need you to hear this as well. James, Aiden, we have a problem. I am down two men. I need to find two more loggers if we are going to get this done in time! James, can we get an extension of a week? We should have your logs by then."

James looked at Patrick and with a semi smile that almost looked like a sneer said, "Patrick, I am going to have to charge you 15% each day you are late. I can't afford it otherwise. The deadline is this coming Monday as you know!"

Patrick looked at Aiden and then at James. He wasn't sure what he was going to do, he would need the men to work 12-hour shifts to get the job completed by the deadline. Considering that some of the loggers like Sam, had been hurt trying to rush the job, safety was just as important as a deadline. The trees were not small, it took a team of 4 to 6 men to cut each tree down, clean, split the logs and send them down river to be floated down to the mill ten miles away!

While James stood at the door of the tent waiting for Patrick to make a decision on how he was going to be able to pay the charges, Aiden said, "Pat...," Patrick looked up.

"Pat, why don't we put an early crew on since it is still light out around 5 am, and have a pm crew work until 8 pm? They can overlap in the afternoon, and we would have more men and stronger teams."

Patrick looked at his logbook then at the deadline. 15% daily would seriously jeopardize his finances at this time. He looked at Aiden, who had just given him a great idea. He would not have to pay his loggers extra for the next week, plus it would be safer if he could get full crews in the middle of the day. Just then, Danny and Bucky came bursting into the camp HQ with news of yet another logger who had been hurt.

"Mr. Smith, I will get you your logs on time and we won't have to pay any charges for being late!" Patrick said as he took Aiden aside and gave a dismissive look to James, who sneered as he left the tent.

Back in town, the Reverend Marshall was at his desk finishing up his ad. He was going to post it in the '*Matrimonial News*' hoping to find a bride that would be his 'helpmate.'

> "*Episcopalian Minister looking for a comely wife, of the same belief. Willing to come out west to wed said Minister. I am 30 years of age, never been married. Would kindly court the young lady, if need be, but would prefer to be married within 6 months of meeting. The young lady should be between the ages of 21 and 25 and be a fairly good housekeeper and cook. I will pay all expenses for travel from your home to Yelm, Washington Territory. Please send picture and description of self. Thank you, The Reverend Oscar C. Marshall.*"

He looked at the envelope. Put his address inside and promptly walked from the church to the mercantile, which was only about a few steps from the church. He stepped inside and handed the envelope to Barney, who was the owner of the Mercantile. Barney and his wife, Emma, were expecting a baby soon.

"Hello, Reverend, what can I do for you?" Barney asked as he carefully measured out the coffee beans for a customer.

"Hello, Barney, how is Emma?"

"Oh, she is doing fine. She said she felt the baby kick just yesterday," Barney replied as he finished tying up the bag of coffee beans.

"I would like to post this letter if it's not too late."

"No problem, Reverend, the stage will be here in about ten minutes, maybe 30 minutes..." Barney left off the rest as he put a stamp on the letter and placed it in the mailbag. Without looking up Barney said, "The Matrimonial News." The reverend looked a little embarrassed but nodded yes.

"Well Reverend, you are not the only one who has sent a letter to that magazine in the past few days. Some of the loggers and millers have done that as well. It won't surprise me if we suddenly have an influx of women coming to this town! Is there anything else?"

The Reverend shook his head and walked out of the mercantile. Patrick almost bumped into the Reverend as he was coming from the other side of the church. Mr. Smith's office was near the saloon, which was right in the middle of the town.

"Excuse me Reverend, but I am in a hurry for a meeting with the council. Are you coming?" Patrick inquired.

"I didn't know there was a council meeting, is this an emergency?"

"Yes, yes, it is!" Patrick hurried past the Reverend, not waiting to see if he was coming. The Reverend followed closely behind and arrived at Mr. Smith's office at the same time as Patrick. They were ushered in where they stood by the wall with Mr. Smith's books and files.

"So glad you could make it O'Donnell!" Mr. Smith said as he offered a drink to those on the council. The reverend looked around and saw that Barney, Aiden, Danny, Josie the saloon owner, and Taylor, who owned the livery stable, were all there.

"I called this meeting today to talk about something of the utmost importance. Pat, you, and your brothers run a fine business, but it can't grow unless we have more men, my milling business is also suffering as well. So, I have a proposal for you. If we get more women in this town, more men will come, and soon we will have a busy town and our businesses will be thriving!" Jim said as he looked around at the others.

Aiden, who was standing by the desk said, "As you know, just because my older brother runs a logging camp doesn't mean I am interested in that as well. I want him to do well enough to hire someone else to do his books!" There was a chuckle among the men. "I was hoping to take the southern 40 acres and start a cattle ranch. There is plenty of land to spread out and raise some beef for market. With the train coming through, I would be able to make a good sale!"

"Yea! What about us farmers?" asked one of the three married men in town. We need land to farm, you don't need to take all of it!"

Aiden looked at him and said, "Henry, you know where I am talking about, we won't be anywhere near your farm!"

There was a murmur in the crowd, and someone said, "What do we need brides for? We can get a dance hall and have them ladies that will bring in other men!" The man laughed along with a couple of his friends as well.

"Fellows, Fellows!" Josie said. Then Danny whistled loudly, and everyone stopped talking to listen.

"I don't mean to put a damper on your ideas, but dance hall girls will not help this town. We need ladies, proper ladies, women with some education and a good upbringing. If you are going to have brides, then you need proper women!" Josie was just about to go on when the Reverend spoke up.

"I guess I am not the only man who has a need for a wife. I sent my letter through to the 'Matrimonial news' and I'm hoping I will hear something soon. Perhaps we can invite a few more ladies to come here?"

Another bit of talking and murmuring ensued, and then Pat said, "Yes, I think we could write an ad and invite a few more ladies, but where will they stay? We haven't got a hotel or boarding house."

They all looked at each other, then Josie spoke up, "Well, Pat, Jim, if your men will build extra rooms, we can have a boarding house/hotel/saloon. But then I would have to charge some kind of rent and maybe the ladies won't have money to pay that rent." She looked around at Pat, Jim, and the others.

The Reverend suggested that the town pool its money to provide for at least 5 'brides' to come, and when they were married, they could invite 5 more. The council thought that was a good idea. They opened up the discussion from the townspeople and everyone agreed to put something in the pot to help fund the ladies who would be coming.

ARRIVAL

It was a bright and sunny summer's day when the ladies arrived in Tacoma. They met on the train from the east, and they were all 'Mail Order Brides.' Some answered ads placed by local men, and some came to find a man. There were 6 ladies in all, ranging from age 17 to 25. There was Beth, age 18 with auburn hair, green eyes, and an Irish lilt still in her voice. Ann had black hair and bright black eyes that shined when she smiled. Nancy and Katie were sisters, both were blonde, but Katie had brown eyes and Nancy had blue eyes. Millie had brown hair and brown eyes, and she was a little shorter than the other ladies. Julie came from South Carolina, and she had a definite southern accent, brown curly hair, and hazel eyes that sparkled when she laughed.

The ladies were on their way to a town called Yelm, in the middle of a prairie. The sisters, Nancy, and Katie had answered an ad from two gentlemen who were farmers/loggers. They hoped the men were kind and good looking. Beth wanted to be married but was also hesitant. Back in the east she had suitors but none of them kindled anything more than friendship. Her parents had 10 children and could not afford her to continue living with them. She was a nanny and used what she earned to go to school. She obtained her teaching degree at the age of 15 but finding a job as a teacher in the east was another story. Her father encouraged her to go to Yelm, so she packed her bag and bought a ticket.

The second Sunday after the women's arrival, there was a church picnic. The Reverend Oscar G. Marshall was one of the men who put an ad in the paper, and he was hoping one of the young ladies would take a liking to him. After church, they all met outside with a table of food for their picnic. At first, the ladies stood on one side of the yard, while the gentlemen stood on the other. Josie and her friend, Sean, decided to get the men and women together.

"Reverend, didn't you write one of those ads? Don't you think you should find out who answered?" Josie asked, smiling at him.

"I suppose..." he started, then he continued, "I suppose you are right Miss LaFleur." He reached into his pocket and found the letter he received from a Miss N. Prescott. Josie took the letter and went over to Nancy. She took Nancy's hand and brought her over to the Reverend.   "Miss Nancy Prescott, meet the Reverend Oscar G. Marshall!" She handed each of them a cup of tea and went over to Katie. She took Katie over to Mr. Robert Taylor, who was the owner of the livery stable. "Miss Katie Prescott, this is Mr. Robert Taylor, he owns the livery stable." She then handed each of them a cup of tea as well and they went off to talk.

Finally, Josie went over to Aiden. She knew the young man; he was like her own son. She took his hand and marched him over to Millie. He wasn't shy but he still wasn't one to go right up to a lady and introduce himself. Josie instinctively knew that these two would be perfect for each other. Aiden was more of a farmer and rancher than his brother, Patrick. He was planning on using most of the acreage they had to farm and raise cattle. Millie told Josie earlier that her family was from Germany and that they had a large farm. "Mr. Aiden O'Donnell, please meet Miss Mildred (Millie) Merz!" She handed them their cups of tea and sent them off to talk.

There was lot of talking going on. James and Patrick had both seen Julie and decided to escort her around to see the sights.

"Why gentlemen, thank you so much for your concern but this lady would like to get to know each of you separately." Julie said in a smooth southern voice. Taking Mr. Smith's arm and with a gentle wave to Patrick, she walked away.

After Patrick excused himself, he saw that his brother Danny was standing by the punch bowl alone.

He went over to him and asked, "Why are you just standing here?"

"Well, no one has introduced me to any of the ladies yet and it seems as if they have all been taken!"

"Danny, you can introduce *yourself* to the other ladies without having someone to introduce you. Josie was just helping the others by introducing them."

Just then, Beth came over to the table and was about to pour herself some punch when Patrick gave Danny a little push and Danny said to her, "May I?" reaching for the cup and the spoon for the punch. "My name is Daniel O'Donnell, but you can call me Danny."

Beth looked at him and said with an air of propriety, "My name is Elizabeth Ann Sweeney, Miss Sweeney to you for now."

"Yes, Miss Sweeney. Here is your cup of punch."

"Thank you, Mr. O'Donnell," she said as she took the cup from him. He could not help but feel that deep down she would be his forever. She also felt the same way but was reluctant to say anything. It would take them a while before they would come to realize they were meant for each other no matter what storms would try to tear them apart.

PART 1
Beth's Nightmare

CHAPTER 1

A couple of years later, Beth was still living in an apartment located off the hotel. Her parents both died in a fire and most of their older siblings had taken in the younger ones, except for the two youngest, Sierra and Michael. Danny, with the help of the loggers, built an extra apartment so Beth and her siblings would be together.

Tomorrow she would finally walk down the aisle. The church had been decorated and Beth had her dress fitting that afternoon and the invitations were sent out. She put her head on the pillow and started to dream of Danny and her together.

The night was quiet, the children and adults were asleep, and even the cattle were lowing. Suddenly, Beth woke up screaming and Sierra ran quickly to her sister. Michael ran after her and they heard what they thought was a loud explosion. Then Josie began to ring the alarm bell, which caused everyone to get up, gather what they needed, and head out to the wagons the loggers brought for them.

A loud roar came from the mountain, it seemed as if it was going to erupt at any moment. The rolling of the earth was not gentle. There was no time to lose as the ladies grabbed what they could carry. At the same time Josie had gone to check on Beth and the children, Beth was coming out of her apartment door with the children carrying a few bags of clothes and necessities.

Patrick and Aiden showed up with a few wagons for the town's people, as well as the new ladies who had arrived just over a week ago. There was another explosion and they all looked toward Mt. Tahoma. It was erupting! Patrick got on his horse and helped get the other animals out of the livery stable. Just then, a third explosion occurred, and this time James Smith went to his mill and asked the single men who worked there to help the ones with families. He looked for his wife, Julie, who had their children wrapped up and, in the wagon, before he knew what was happening.

"Jim, I have your books and accounts, the children and I will get out of town and head toward Lacey, I think that will be far enough." Julie said to James. He looked at her and thought, yes, he had made the right decision to marry her a few years back. She was definitely the woman, wife, and mother for him.

"Thank you, Julie. I will stay and help who I can."

"That is fine, I will meet you at our friend's house in Lacey, but please don't get hurt!"

Julie pleaded as she gave him a quick kiss and started to leave in the wagon.

Patrick helped round up the animals and they were going to head toward Lacey as well. Aiden's wife already moved their cattle and children away from the erupting mountain. When they met, Patrick and Aiden looked at each other and wondered where Danny had been or where he was. The Reverend Marshall and Nancy were gathering their children as well as helping the neighbors. Patrick passed the Reverend and asked:

"Reverend, have you seen Danny?" Patrick shouted as another loud belch from the fiery volcano burst out from the top.

"I saw him on his horse. He said he was headed to the outlying areas to see if he could help the families out there, as well as the Indian tribe nearby!"

Patrick thanked the Reverend as he and Aiden got on their horses. Aiden shouted to his brother, "Pat, do you want me to go look for Danny?" Patrick looked at him with worry in his eyes. He was concerned for his brother, but he knew he still needed Aiden to help with those people who were trying to get out of town.

"No Aiden, I think he will be all right, however, keep an eye out for him. I am going to the other end of town to check the buildings. I don't think there was anyone in the jail, but I want to be sure."

As Patrick headed toward the end of town, Aiden did a sweep of the hotel and offices. He grabbed what he could of their business transactions, but just then the earth shook, and a lamp fell and started a fire. Aiden's horse reared up and was about to run, then Aiden jumped on his back, and they took off toward the other end of town. Patrick fared no better because his horse almost bucked him off to run, but Patrick was capable, confident, and in control, "Calm down now Whiskey, that's a good boy...," he whispered in the horse's ear as he put half a cloth on one side of the horse's eyes and the other half on the other side. "Let's go now Whiskey," he said calmly but firmly, kicking the horse slightly as they headed back the way they came.

CHAPTER 2

They arrived in Lacey by midnight and the town was fairly quiet. The earthquakes and explosions from the mountain hadn't woken the people of the town. In fact, no one was available when they arrived at the edge of town. They decided to park themselves in a small clearing to rest and get some sleep. Some of the children were still sleeping but Beth, her sister, her brother, and a few others were still awake.

Beth hadn't seen Danny and wondered what happened to him. She walked over to Josie and Sean and asked them if they had seen Danny.

Sean answered as he was helping Josie down from the wagon seat, "I think I saw him heading out of town the back way, it looked like he was going to check on some of those farmers and people who live a little closer to the mountain"

Linda, one of the new brides, came up to ask what she could do to help. "I can cook, clean, and watch the littluns," she said. She had come from the Appalachians and still had her accent.

"Linda, we may need your help in that department soon enough. Do you think you could lay down for a little while and get some sleep?" asked Josie. Linda looked at Josie and Beth then shook her head yes. She was still so much a child but willing to do adult things if needed.

"She is a good girl. She will make someone a good wife," Beth said. Josie looked at Beth and saw that she was staring out across the vast prairie in the early morning hours. Beth was hoping to see some sign, a lone rider perhaps, that was Danny.

Patrick saw to the settling and was planning to go to the nearest hotel to find out if they could get places to stay for some of the families. Jackson, one of the loggers that worked for Patrick, said he and his family had relatives nearby and they would stay with them for a while. He would get word to Patrick when they were settled and let him know if there would be room for a few more families to stay with his relatives. Later, as the sun came up in the East, many of the people from Yelm, looked toward the mountain and it was still spitting fire and smoke but seemed to have calmed down a bit.

Josie spoke with the hotel proprietor and made arrangements for Sean and her to provide supplies to those families that would be camping out nearby. Beth was troubled but tried not to show it. She thought to herself, 'Danny and I have been planning to get married and each time something happens to postpone it. It seems as if we aren't meant to be married!' She started to cry and looked toward the mountain as she wondered if he had been swallowed up by the volcano.

"Beth, Beth!" shouted Sierra, who had come to see her sister by their wagon. Beth stood up and looked at Sierra, then hugged her.

"What is it?"

"There is word that we might be moving back soon. It has been a week now...You've been crying."

Beth nodded, then Michael came storming in and interrupted the conversation. "Beth, Sierra. Mr. Pat says that we will be returning soon! Isn't that great?!" Michael looked at Sierra and Beth and he noticed something wrong with Beth's eyes. "You're crying, I'm so sorry." Michael stood there not quite knowing what to do.

Patrick, Aiden, and Mr. Smith were in the tent when a visitor arrived. Patrick stood up and went over to the visitor who said, "Patrick O'Donnell, you must come with me!"

"Sleeping Fox, I am glad to see you, has your tribe survived? Have you seen Danny?" Aiden said standing with the others to greet Sleeping Fox.

"I think so. We have seen someone who looks like him. He was hurt and we have cared for him for a week, but now he doesn't seem to know who he is.

Please come with me." Sleeping Fox began to leave but saw that James and Aiden were beginning to follow them. "They cannot follow, it is only you we will talk to, Patrick O'Donnell!"

James looked at Patrick, then Patrick said to Sleeping Fox, "Mr. Smith here is also a chief in our village, may he not come along?" Sleeping Fox looked at them, nodded in favor and waited for the horses to be readied.

Patrick and James were ready to leave. Patrick told Aiden to keep things quiet. He asked Aiden not to say anything, except that they would be back soon. Patrick and James got on their horses and rode out with Sleeping Fox. Josie saw them leaving and asked Aiden what was going on. Aiden said that they would be back soon. Josie looked at Aiden with curiosity but didn't pursue it any further.

Just above on a hill, sat a man on his horse, observing the goings and comings of the little band of people in the clearing. He wasn't quite sure who they were. When two children noticed him, he hurriedly turned his horse and went down the opposite side of the hill.

Chapter 3

Beth had been sleeping fitfully and Nancy, now Mrs. Reverend Marshall, was sitting with her that evening. Josie came by later in the night and sat with Beth until morning. Katie also came by in the morning. During one of her restless half sleep/half-awake moments, Beth started to cry out, "Danny, Danny, I can't find you, where are you?!" She tossed and turned so much that she almost fell off her cot. Josie got her back on the cot and when she awoke, she sat up eyes staring forward, and shouted, "Danny, I am right here near the tree, just look, look at me, you will know who I am!"

"Beth, Beth, wake up! Wake up!" Josie said loudly as she shook her a little. Finally, Beth woke up, looked at Josie and started to cry. "It's okay, Beth, I'm here." Josie was holding Beth's head on her shoulder.

"Oh, Josie, I dreamt that Danny was standing by a tree, and he didn't see me! I was calling to him, but he couldn't hear me! Oh Josie, what if I have lost him forever!!!" Beth cried some more while Josie soothed her.

Early in the morning Josei went to see Emma to ask if Beth could take care of little Barney Jr. Emma was not too excited but after Josie explained to Emma that having Beth to help with the new baby would also help Beth.

Emma said: "Well, it is true that I do need a little rest and Barney Sr. is not able to help right now because he has to be at the store..." she trailed off for a moment then said yes to Josie and they went to the hotel with everything that was needed to care for a baby. Beth took the baby and promised she would care for him while Emma got some rest. Beth was still sobbing quietly, but now she had something to keep her mind busy. Taking care of the baby soothed her and made her happy for a little while. Karen, one of the brides who had not married yet, was also there doing some sewing just outside the wagon where Beth was staying.

As Josie and Emma were walking towards Emma's and Barney's wagon. Karen came running up to them with Emma's baby and said:

"Don't let Beth have the baby anymore!" Karen shouted.

Both Dr. Lynne and Aiden arrived upon the scene and Aiden asked, "What is happening here?" Karen explained that Beth had been playing with the baby when she suddenly almost dropped the baby on the floor! Karen caught the baby and saw a wild look in

Beth's eyes. Karen then ran out and gave the baby to Emma. During the explanation, Beth came out of the wagon hollering about not letting anyone take the baby away from her. Her eyes looked wild, and she seemed very confused. Dr. Lynne came up to her and gently calmed her down. She got Beth back in the wagon and gave her a sedative.

The doctor came out and said to Aiden and Josie, "Beth has not been sleeping well, so I gave her a mild sedative. I don't want her to be alone. I would like to know if one of you ladies, or all of you ladies, can take turns watching her. Sierra and Michael may have to stay with other friends until I feel she is getting better. She needs more sleep and a routine. If she doesn't calm down by next week, or if she still isn't sleeping, we can try a little laudanum, but that hopefully won't be needed." Dr. Lynne then left to go see a couple more patients.

Aiden walked away and found a tree stump to sit on. He was feeling overwhelmed and needed Patrick and to some extent Danny to help with dealing with the issues of this town. Mr. Smith was okay, but it wasn't the same. The O'Donnell brothers were very close! He put his hands on his head and began to cry silently. Karen was still upset so she decided to take a walk. When she came back, she saw Aiden on the tree stump, and she walked over to him. Aiden lifted his head as Karen knelt down beside him and they held each other for a long time.

The stranger on the horse stood on top of a nearby hill and watched all that was going on. He couldn't determine who the people were at the bottom of the hill. He wanted to go down to see if he knew who they were, but he felt he couldn't, so he slowly turned and went to his own camp in the hills; a place he had known since he was a boy.

CHAPTER 4

The meeting at the Indian encampment cleared up many questions Patrick and James had about the destruction of their beloved city. They knew they would have to rebuild and with their friends and the rest of the town, they knew they could rebuild. But for now, they would have to live in the camp until the city was rebuilt. They said goodbye to Sleeping Fox and headed back to the camp.

Patrick and James were walking their horses and talking about the information they received from the Indians. "You know, Pat, this rebuilding project will take a while to complete," James said.

Patrick sat on his horse thinking. He was always thinking. Then he said, "With your mill and our lumber, we can get the town built within a month. Most of the houses are intact and some of the families can move back to their homes if they want to."

"The question is will they want to, Pat? It is going to take a lot of work and money and I'm not sure we have enough money to do it," James interjected as they crossed a little creek heading back toward Lacey.

"Well, I do have an idea, but we will have to talk to everyone in the camp. I know some of the loggers will be willing to help, we just have to hope the families are willing to stay." The kept plodding along as they got closer and closer to Lacey.

"They're back! They're back!" Michael called out as he and Sierra were finishing some chores. They ran over to Patrick and James and said, "Patrick, we think Danny has been watching us. We told Josie and she told Aiden. There is a man up on the hill and he's been watching us from his horse!" Patrick smiled and got off his horse. He asked Michael and Sierra what they meant when they said someone was watching them. James got down as well and looked at Patrick.

"I will check into that, meanwhile I need to see Aiden and Beth!"

James and Patrick decided to get cleaned up and get something to eat, and they would meet with the townspeople later. James said he was going to check with Jack about his mill workers, and Patrick went directly to see Aiden and Beth. He noticed that Josie and Nancy were coming over to him.

"Oh Patrick, thank God you are back! Beth has been having an awful time and we wanted to know where Danny was. We also want to know about going back to Yelm." Nancy said. By the look in Aiden's eyes, Patrick had more to worry about.

"Nancy, can you bring Beth into the tent please?"

Aiden jumped in and said, "No, Nancy don't bring Beth just yet, I need to tell Patrick what has happened with her." Patrick looked at Aiden, who nodded and mouthed 'later.'

After James and Patrick had their supper and were rested, they called Barney, Josie, and Aiden together to discuss what the Indians had said to them. James began by saying, "When we sat with the other tribes, we listened to what they had to say. It seems as if there was some sort of 'fire from the sky' that rained down on our area of the planet a week ago. The tribes believe it was an ominous sign and indeed for us it was. They said they didn't know this would happen. They had seen many of these over the course of the years and yet there has been nothing that they have seen to make it happen like it did. If they had known, they would have told us."

"So, James, you are saying that not telling us was not their fault?!" Barney said.

"No, what they were telling us is that if they would have had any indication, they would have said something. They themselves suffered some problems and they had to leave their village the same night we left ours."

Patrick spoke up, "We know that when a volcano explodes, it can send out fireballs. They said this hasn't happened before." Barney seemed to understand better and sat down. After the meeting, Patrick and James called the entire town to discuss what happened and what the plans were to rebuild.

Aiden pulled Patrick aside and asked what they were going to do with Beth and how they were going to tell her what happened to Danny. "I don't know yet. I have asked Nancy and Josie to watch her and the other girls as well. But I'm not sure she is ready to hear what happened to Danny."

Barney was nearby and asked, "Just what has happened to Danny?"

"He has lost his memory. We have to ask Dr. Lynne what we can do." Patrick replied.

"Well, what are we going to do about Danny? He is out there wandering around and not sure about who he is. He may be dangerous now. It seems he could do some serious damage if he isn't in his right mind." Barney said anxiously.

"I have asked Dr. Lynne and Miss Etta to go to Tacoma and wire Sean in San Francisco to find a doctor to help Danny. At least maybe we can get some ideas on what we can and cannot do. Dr. Lynne says his memory will improve over time, but he needs to be somewhere he is familiar with."

"Meanwhile, how do we keep Beth from over-doing the laudanum? If Danny gets his memory back, I don't think he will want to see Beth addicted to that stuff." Aiden asked. Just then, Josie, Karen, and Nancy came in.

"Beth will not be addicted; I will not let her!" Josie said as Karen agreed. Nancy, who was there to find out what to do, just nodded in agreement.

"How do you know Josie?" Patrick asked.

"I have seen my share of young girls addicted to that. In fact, there is one girl I remember, who now has moved on. She was one of the girls who seemed to get too attached to certain things that were not good for her!" Josie stopped and then said, "No, Beth is not that kind of girl. She is in love and is grieving for Danny, but she will not become addicted. It may take some time but with my help and the other ladies help, we will keep her healthy for when Danny returns!" Patrick looked at Josie and was grateful that she was truly a mother to the O'Donnell's, as well as all the girls. He gave Josie a generous hug and then said they needed to talk to the town.

CHAPTER 5

I t had been several weeks, in fact almost a month since the events that destroyed their town and their lives. James and Patrick worked hard alongside the rest of the town to rebuild. Josie's saloon was up and running, and since Sean had managed to save the important items, she was able to start making money to purchase some new decorations and furnishings for her place.

"Well, Josie my dear, I think we have done a fantastic job!" Sean said as he drank a draught of his 'good Irish whiskey!

"Sean, I can't thank you enough for saving our supply, but that does not mean you have free drinks every time you come here!" Sean laughed and then kissed Josie on the cheek as he left. Josie just looked at him and sighed. James walked in to get lunch and Patrick came in after him.

"You know Patrick, if you cut that timber on the south ridge this week, we can have it ready for you in two weeks." James said. James was proud of his sawmill, and he had decided to be a benefactor for a new young artist. He was a wood carver who had come into town a week ago and showed everyone that he was a real artist and wanted to start a business there. So, James gave him a place to work, and now Barney's Mercantile was a 'showroom' for his interesting pieces of art.

"About that, I will have my loggers cut that for you, but Aiden and I want to find Danny. I know he's still out there and I was hoping his memory would come back sooner than this. Dr. Lynne said it takes time to recover, but how long? She never gave me an answer."

"Patrick, if you no longer have your foreman, I think Aiden should stay here to run the business while you go off chasing your brother! I mean, you want to keep your mountain and your business, don't you?" James was worried that the best business partner he had wouldn't be around to help get the project done in time. He and Patrick had a 'love-hate' relationship in business. Sometimes they supported each and other times they were against each other. Patrick looked at James and almost took what he said as an insult, but instead of reacting instinctively he just put the thought away until another day. This was not the time to waste on useless arguments or insults.

Patrick took a bite of his steak and said, "I know we lost Rusty Arnold during the eruption, but I have asked someone else. Mark Jensen said he would do it and accepted the offer to come back on a temporary basis until we can hire a new foreman. Jensen will oversee the operation and Miss Etta will be teaching school again, along with Miss Darla Hansen. So, there is no problem for Aiden and me to take time to go looking for our brother."

James nodded. Mark Jenson had been a logger when the O'Donnell family had first started. He had worked for their dad but decided to move away to start a family and have a farm. As for Danny, James knew the real reason they needed to find Danny. It seems as if Beth, as strong as she was had been totally devastated and everyone was worried about her. If Danny didn't come back or if he had died, they were afraid she would need specialized help. "Okay, I see your point. Well, I do hope you find him. Danny was/is the better part of the O'Donnell brothers!" James said with a smirky smile on his face as he finished the last bite of his lunch.

When they rebuilt the hotel and Josie's saloon, they decided to attach the hotel to the saloon. Karen was now running the hotel, and since she was a good organizer, she was the best manager for the position. Beth, Linda, and a few of the girls who had just arrived after the disaster were all involved. They would cook, clean, and keep the rooms spotless. They all helped.

"Josie, when you place orders the next time, please include at least two more sets of sheets. I don't know what one person did, but if he doesn't stop coming here and ruining our sheets, we are going to have ask him to buy his own!" Karen said jokingly.

"I will put that down on my list, thank you Karen!" Josie replied as she was going over the registration for the hotel, then she continued, "Karen, Mr. Harmon will be coming any day now and he wants Suite 104, and he has asked to use the event room for a party next Tuesday evening."

Karen acknowledged the request but remembered they had a women's club meeting on the same day. "I think we have a women's club meeting on that day around 2:00. Will there be enough time to clean and prepare for the party?" Josie said yes and asked if she had seen Beth. Karen shook her head and left.

Not long after, Beth and Dr. Lynne came into the hotel laughing and smiling. "My, what have we here, a happy Beth? And Dr. Lynne so good of you to come over." Josie said, seeming concerned about Beth's current state of mind.

Dr. Lynne and Beth finished their conversation and Beth walked off to her room. Dr. Lynne walked over to Josie and said, "Josie she is getting surer of herself, but she is still fragile. I would like you to keep the Laudanum somewhere she won't find it, but if she realty needs it, I know you are particularly good friends with her, and I can rest assured that you will know the right time to give it to her." Josie nodded to Dr. Lynne, took the bottle, and put it in her pocket.

"Is she really getting better? Do you think she will have a relapse?"

"I'm not sure about the relapse, but as the days go by, she has been doing better. She is helping Miss Etta with plans for the next school term and Miss Etta thinks she can get a teacher license for her. That will help a whole lot. She will be too busy to think about you know who and she will be happy with the children at the school. I have some other patients to see. If you need to go somewhere, please let Karen or one of the other ladies know so that Beth doesn't panic."

Dr. Lynne left and Josie remembered the few weeks that had just passed. Almost daily they would find Beth in the O'Donnell cabin, or near their favorite rock or picnic site. One day, they could not find her at all, until late in the evening when she came walking back to town. She had been saying some confusing things that evening. She even said she met Danny, and he was coming to get her as soon as he could. No one believed her. The townspeople thought he had died. Only Patrick, Aiden, James, Dr. Lynne, and Josie knew he was alive, but for Beth's sake they couldn't let her know, not yet anyway.

The new artist/wood carver's name was Jacques Luis Le Beau. His business was doing a great and he was contracted out by a few of the wealthier people who had moved to Yelm but lived closer to the University. They liked to have pleasant things and since they had enough money, they invested in those things. He was tall, dark, and handsome and he spoke multiple languages, including some Indian languages. He was originally from Québec, Canada but found that the Washington territory/state was much more to his liking. He was older than most of the young ladies who were in the dormitory, but he didn't have a problem if they didn't.

There was one young lady who always seemed so sad, and he decided to cheer her up with some flowers and sometimes a piece of a French pastry. His father had been a baker, so he had picked up a few recipes. His attitude was that he could catch more women with French pastry than flies. He was always joking and laughing, and he was a promising investment for Yelm's future, as well as Mr. Smith's businesses.

Although Jacques was not in a sense 'courting' any one woman, he was enchanted with one or two girls in the group at the hotel. Since there were no women of the 'lower sort' to be with, he learned to hone his skills with the ladies from the East and other parts. One day, he was coming out of the hotel with his hat in his hand and was about to walk to the mercantile when he saw Beth leaving the hotel by another door.

He knew she tended to disappear and worried the others, so he thought he could go to the mercantile another day and decided to follow her.

She walked up the hill past the outskirts of town and went to the cemetery with some flowers for a grave. When she was told that Danny had died, she insisted on having a gravestone made for him so she could go and sit and talk to him. Patrick made a Bench, and Aiden purchased a stone for the 'imaginary' grave. "Oh, Danny, what am I to do? My life has stopped, and I can't go on. Why can't you come back to me?! I hate it here without you!" She buried her face in her hands and cried.

Jacques came upon Beth and saw her crying. He reached for a handkerchief to help her dry her tears. "Excuse me, mademoiselle. I was just wondering if I might be of any help or comfort to you in your time of grief?" He handed her is handkerchief and she dried her eyes. She looked so sad.

He reached out to hold her in his arms and she let him. Beth looked at him, as if she were still in a dream. Then she pulled back from his arms and said, "That is quite all right, I am okay now. You must be the gentleman caller who has been leaving me flowers and pastries. I must tell you that my heart belongs to another, and he may be gone but I am still his." Jacques did not want to hint at something that probably would upset her.

"My dear lady, I have meant nothing by my little gifts. I was hoping to see you happy as you were before. Would you like to talk about your love? Sometimes talking about it helps the grief to heal." She looked at him and thanked him. All she wanted to do was go back to town before anyone missed her. He asked if he could walk with her and she said yes, but nothing else during the walk.

Edith and Edna, two spinster sisters who were considered the town gossips, were on their porch having an afternoon tea when they saw Beth with the artist. "Well! Would you look at that, I thought she was mourning the loss of her beau, Danny O'Donnell! Here she is just walking with another man so soon after his death! What a scandal!" Edna said snidely.

"Yes, it is a scandal, we need to see James right away! Oh, Michael, would you go tell James that we need to talk to him as soon as possible? Here is a quarter for doing that errand!" Edith said.

"Thank you, ma'am." Michael said as he scurried off to James' office at the mill.

CHAPTER 6

Patrick and Aiden made it to Sleeping Fox's camp where they were greeted by one of the other sub chiefs of the tribe and given food and drink. Soon, Sleeping Fox returned and after having refreshed himself, he met with Patrick and Aiden.

"Patrick O'Donnell, your brother has been well physically, but he still has not remembered who he is. He walks these mountains but does so as a spirit missing his body." Sleeping Fox paused and then said, "When we first met, Patrick O'Donnell, you said your brother was not quite all the way there. I believed that Patrick O'Donnell, until these past few days. He came to warn us, and as he was warning us when the earthquake hit. He was thrown from his horse and landed head first. I sent my women to help him, since we knew who he was. We took care of him and then when he was healthy, we said he should return to his home. That is when he looked at us and did not realize he was not home. He muttered something about his mother will be missing him. We did not comment and just gave him some new clothes and his horse. My shaman said that he may remember someday, but we do not know. Now he walks these mountains in search of himself."

Patrick looked at Aiden, both were worried. "Do you know where we might find him? We came to bring him home." asked Aiden, his blue eyes full of worry for his brother.

"He walks this mountain, he has camped, hunted, and fished, but never goes towards his home. As I said, he is like a spirit who is looking for his home!"

Patrick thought more about this, then he said, "Thank you for telling us, Sleeping Fox. We appreciate all that you have done. Please let us know if you need any help at all!" Sleeping Fox stood up and the meeting was ended.

"Go in peace and find your brother, his spirit may yet be saved!" Sleeping Fox exclaimed as he raised his hand. Both Aiden and Patrick nodded and left on their horses.

Patrick stopped Aiden when they were far away from the camp and said, "Aiden, you go back to town, and I am going to find Danny and see if he will come back with me. He may or he may not, but I must try. I will see you in a few days."

"Patrick, it has been over a month, will he remember anything at all?"

"I don't know Aiden, but I am going to take him to our family cabin and see if it helps him at all." Aiden continued his ride into town and Patrick went further up the mountain.

Danny was sitting at his camp. It was evening and he had found some good trout for dinner. He sat and ate in silence until he heard footsteps. He quickly doused the fire, then hid behind a rock. He had a knife and a bow and arrow the Indians gave him when he left their village. They had been very friendly to him, and he thought they were his people. The shaman said he came from somewhere else and had to leave to find out where he came from. Danny hadn't gone any farther; he stayed there, close to the village. He felt a sort of peace and safety where he was, at least until now.

Hiding behind the rock, Danny waited until he saw a shadow and without hesitation, he jumped onto the man and was about to kill him. The man overpowered him, knocked him on his back and would not let him get up. The man tossed the dropped knife and pinned Danny down so he couldn't get up. "Who are you? Let me go! I will kill you!" Danny yelled.

"Danny, Danny, it is me, Patrick!" Danny didn't respond to his name or to Patrick's name either. "Danny, if you promise to sit up and hear me out, I will let you go?" Danny's wild blue eyes looked at Patrick, who was still pinning him down. In the dark he couldn't tell, but something deep inside seemed vaguely familiar. Danny nodded his assent and Patrick got off and moved back, waiting to see what Danny would do. They both sat, staring at each other until Patrick said, "I think we should light a fire so we can at least see each other." Danny nodded and lit the fire.

Once the fire was going, they both sat across from each other and Danny watched Patrick warily. "Who are you?" Danny asked.

"I am your brother, Patrick."

"P-p-Patrick? I don't know that name. I don't know my name either, but you say it is D-d-Danny?"

"Yes, it is! There was an explosion and we all left Yelm in a hurry, and you went to warn the others!" Danny looked at him, his head was spinning with this revelation.

"I-I-I live in a place called Yelm?" Danny inquired. He shook his head and suddenly felt faint and started to fall over. Patrick caught him, laid him down gently and covered him up with blankets and let him sleep. Patrick sat by a tree watching and praying for his brother.

The next morning, Patrick made some breakfast for him and Danny. When Danny woke up, he was pleasantly surprised that Patrick was so kind and had made breakfast, but he was still wary. "Well, good morning. I am sorry we don't have any coffee, but I made some hot tea from your tea leaves." Patrick said as he offered a cup to Danny. Danny took it gratefully and sipped it slowly.

Danny was eyeing Patrick because he wasn't sure if he was telling him the truth, so he said to Patrick, "Ah! Mister?"

"Call me Patrick!"

"Patrick, do you mind not calling me Danny? I don't seem to recall or have any special feeling for that name. Could you call me Ian?" Danny requested. Patrick heard that name, smiled, and thought to himself, 'yes, he does remember something, even if he doesn't know it.'

"Sure, I can call you Ian." Danny (now known as Ian) smiled at Patrick, and they ate a little breakfast.

"Ian, would you like to come to Yelm? It is a Beautiful town. There are many who know of you and would like to see you."

Ian thought for a while and replied, "Yes, sure that will be fine. I have some furs to sell. Do you know by chance if anyone in town buys furs?"

"Yes, they sure do," Patrick replied as they finished packing up their things.

After they finished packing up their things, Ian and Patrick headed to Yelm. Patrick thought he might take Ian to the cabin but decided to wait to see what the doctor would say first.

CHAPTER 7

Patrick and Ian entered Yelm and the first ones to see them were James and Barney. They both smiled, but were curious, and thought, 'was this real Danny?' Ian had a beard and looked a bit scruffy. Patrick took him to Josie's saloon and with a booming voice Patrick said to everyone before they could say anything, "Folks, while looking for Danny, I found this young man who might know where Danny is. His name is Ian!" Everyone looked a little confused but then Jensen said, "Hello Ian!" Then everyone else started to call him Ian.

Beth heard that Patrick was back and went to the saloon to find out. When she saw him, she was a little confused. He sorts of looked like Danny, but his name was Ian. Timidly, she said, "Hello, Ian. It's nice to meet you!" When she reached out to shake his hand, she suddenly felt dizzy and was about to faint when Jacques stepped up to steady her. Jacques took Beth to a chair and Nancy came over to sit with her.

Dr. Lynne had just walked in and told Nancy to take Beth back to the hotel.

"Hello Ian, my name is Dr. Lynne, it is a pleasure to meet you!" Ian smiled and nodded his head. Josie came over to him and said, "Sir, would you like a room for the night? Perhaps a bath and a shave as well?" Ian said that would be fine. In fact, he asked if there were any good barbers in town because he wanted to shave off his beard. Josie said yes and gave him a room key. Patrick smiled as Ian left to go to his hotel room.

"Patrick, do you know that what you are doing may be considered dishonest? He still doesn't know who he is. I can tell by the look in his eyes. You may be playing with fire!" Dr. Lynne warned. Patrick looked at Dr. Lynne and the rest of the town's people that were in the saloon. He quietly asked everyone to play along as if Danny was Ian. After all, Ian O'Donnell was their father and if he has a little memory of that, then he may start to gain all of his memories back by just being in town. "Patrick, sometimes I wonder who the doctor is here." Dr. Lynne said with a smile.

After Ian had a bath, Josie helped him shave. He felt good and was ready to go into town to find someone who would buy his furs. Meanwhile, Beth was in her room and Karen was sitting with her when the doctor came in. "Well, how are you, Beth?" Doctor Lynne asked.

"I don't know, he looks so much like Danny, I am afraid to ask him."

"Beth, I know this is a shock to you, but it is Danny! But until he regains his memories, he thinks he is someone else."

"I have to go to him! I have to see him!"

"Not yet Beth, not yet. Remember he doesn't have his memory back so he may not react well to you, or he may have a relapse and never remember."

Beth was surprised by Dr. Lynne's response and said, "So, I have to play along until he regains his memories?"

"Yes, but there is something else. He has shaved and cleaned up and now he looks like Danny again. I want you to be strong and when you go out in public, wait until he approaches you. Don't approach him and be sure to call him Ian."

"That was his father's name!"

"Yes, it was, and he seems to remember that. Anything else will have to wait until he remembers himself." Dr. Lynne looked at Beth with compassion and hoped she would be okay when she saw Danny again now that he was all cleaned up.

Dr. Lynne left, and Beth and Karen looked at each other. "What are you thinking Karen?"

"Oh, nothing, nothing at all."

"You are thinking of something, tell me!"

"Well, I just thought that, well, the doctor said not to hurry though." Karen said as she was trying to stall the conversation. Beth gave her that look. Karen knew she had to say what was on her mind and continued, "Well, maybe after he has been here for a while, we could get you two together for a special dinner and he would remember you. That's all."

"Karen that is a very nice idea, but I think we should wait until he has gotten used to the town and us before we do that." Karen nodded and they both decided to wait.

PART 2
DANNY'S DREAM

CHAPTER 1

Danny woke up unaware of where he was for a little while. He sat up and rubbed his head, realizing there was a large bump on the back of it. He put his hands down and wondered what happened. He couldn't remember what happened, but he was somewhere out on a prairie. He looked around to see if there was anyone or anything that was familiar to him. He saw trees and bushes, but no water that he could see. He stood up and brushed himself off. As he placed his hands on his face, he felt stubble growing and thought that maybe he should find himself a place to clean up. He saw a horse in the distance, and he wondered if it was his horse. He decided to check it out.

Danny started walking toward the horse and he stumbled a little and fell. He stood up and again walked toward the horse. When he got to the horse it had a saddle and also water, which is what he was so badly in need of. He drank the water, then he looked on the saddle for any kind of identification.

He looked in the bags and found nothing that with a name on it, but he did find initials on the saddle which read 'IDO.' He wondered what 'IDO' stood for. Was that his initials? Would the horse let him ride?

The horse seemed to know him, so Danny tried to mount it. As he grabbed onto the horn of the saddle, the horse walked away. Danny was confused but he looked at the horse and then tried again. This time the horse stayed still until he was halfway mounted, then the horse jolted forward and ran while he fell to the ground again. Danny was starting to get frustrated. This time, instead of mounting the horse, he took the reins and walked with the horse, talking, and whispering words until he came to a large rock. Holding onto the reigns, Danny mounted the horse from on top of the rock and the horse stayed still. The horse waited for direction from Danny, then when he pulled on the reigns the horse started to walk.

Danny looked up at the sky and saw that it was nearly nightfall. He heard voices and wondered if they were friendly or not. He dismounted the horse and crept quietly to a campfire where he heard the voices better. "Well, I'll tell you pal," said one of the men, "that earthquake sure was a shaker, split the earth in two! Now, over yonder there's a new cliff and a deep ravine about a mile wide!"

"Yea, I know, scare't my horse so bad he ran off! Haven't seen him since! But I did see a horse down in the prairie, maybe I'll go see if he might be mine!" the other man said.

A third man spit into the fire and said, "I think I might just go and see what is left of that town. I heard the ladies, I mean them brides, might have been left to fend for themselves and we might each get at least one or two for the takin"

The two other men sat and thought a minute about that. They thought perhaps that would be a good idea. "I heard the men just ran off and left them ladies there, so I suppose if we come in to rescue them, they'll give us a reward or something like that!" The men all laughed at that.

Meanwhile, Danny sat back and wondered why the ladies about whom they were talking sounded familiar. He couldn't quite put his finger on it just yet. He also didn't want to go into the camp because he didn't have any kind of weapon to protect himself. He thought it would be a good thing to walk away quietly so they wouldn't know he had even been there. Danny backed off and walked the horse to the other side of the hill where the others had been camped. He laid down in a crevasse of a rock after securing the horse, who now seemed to be content with him, and he fell asleep right away. By the time he woke, the sun was already very high in the sky. Danny already decided to find this town of which he had heard. They hadn't said the name, but he was sure he would find it.

About a few miles into the densely forested mountain, the natives were getting ready to leave. They had survived the earthquake, thanks to Danny O'Donnell, the youngest O'Donnell brother. They believed he was crazy, or some believed that. The chief knew otherwise and hadn't said anything when he had the O'Donnell brothers and their wives at his camp. "Come, you three scout out where we can find some food. We will be travelling toward the prairie today," the chief said to his braves. Then he set about making sure everyone was ready to travel.

The scouts headed out and down the mountain toward the prairie. They set their sights toward the rising sun and looked for evidence of a stream or river to follow, since that would provide some food for the tribe. Along the way, they saw three men traveling, two were on horseback headed toward the town of Yelm. They watched silently as the men headed right past them, not realizing that they were only just a few feet away. One of the scouts wanted to attack, but another said, "Not today, maybe another." After the three white men rode off, they followed a path more inland than usual. It was getting late in the day and their tribe would be arriving soon, so they would camp for the night. They suddenly heard a noise and a rustling in the bushes. Quickly they hid but had their bow and arrows out just in case.

Danny came out from behind the large bush, looking lost and confused and very uncomfortable. He didn't seem to know which way to go. He knew it was getting late and he should stop for the night, but he wasn't sure where he was going or where he would find some food. The horse would stop occasionally and eat some grass, but it seemed ok. Danny also knew he had to find water. He was weary and tired, so he decided to stop at a tree. The tree reminded him of something, but he wasn't sure what it was. He made a little campfire and looked around a bit for food. The scouts watched Danny for a bit. They realized the whole tribe would be upon them soon, so they decided to 'capture' him for the chief. As Danny set up his camp, the scouts slowly crept up to him, grabbed him, tied him up, and gagged him. They were congratulating themselves as the rest of the tribe showed up, and they all decided to stop and camp for the night. When the chief saw Danny, he went up to the scouts and said, "What have you done?! Untie him and give him some food!" he commanded. Then he told the scouts he would talk to them later as he proceeded to help Danny. "Thank you!" Danny said. His voice was familiar to the chief, but the chief said nothing. Danny sat where he was told and did not argue when they brought him food and water. After the chief had dispensed punishment on the scouts, he invited Danny into his tent. They smoked a pipe and Danny seemed to feel like he was spinning, then he dropped on the floor. The chief smiled because he knew exactly who Danny was, but he also knew that something wasn't right with him. He placed Danny in the corner of his teepee and had one of his wives sit with him. They would feed him and care for him until he was better.

CHAPTER 2

D anny had been the chief's guest for more than a few days. Not necessarily an uninvited guest, but a guest, nevertheless. He sent one of his scouts to where the O'Donnell's and the town's people were camping while they were rebuilding Yelm. When the scout came back, he brought word that Patrick would be traveling to see them within a few days. The chief thought this was good, since he knew that the boys' older brothers would know more about how to care for him. Danny had been sleeping and had a fever until a few days ago, when he finally started to feel better. Patrick and Aiden didn't get there for another week, and by then Danny had left the native's camp. Danny decided that although he didn't have an identity, he didn't feel right having the natives take care of him. He remembered the initials on the horse's saddle and thought it meant his first name was something like Ian. He told the natives to call him Ian and he left after thanking them for taking care of him.

Patrick and Aiden arrived the day after Danny (Ian) had left. They enjoyed a meal and visited with the chief. "It is time!" said chief Sleeping Fox. "Patrick O'Donnell, Aiden O'Donnell, your brother has no memory of who he is. That is perhaps because we think he took a fall after he came to warn us to move. We are grateful to him, so when we found him, we took care of him. Our shaman has also looked after him and he says it is not unusual for a man to forget himself if he has hit his head hard enough." Patrick kept silent and motioned for Aiden to keep silent as well. The chief continued, "He has left our camp but there is a brave who is following him to ensure he will be okay. I do not believe he is 'crazy,' but I do believe he has a simple spirit who has captured his mind, and when he is healed by your white powers, he will remember who he is. Until then, we will keep an eye on him since he has helped us, and we will help him." The chief nodded to Patrick that it was his turn to speak.

"Thank you chief, I am glad you found our brother. I am planning to take him home. Our doctor said that she will help him get better."

"Patrick O'Donnell, we let your brother go not because we would not help him here, but because he does not know who he is, and we cannot give that information to him. Only you and yours can do that!"

Aiden spoke up and said, "I think if he is in surroundings where he is familiar, he will recover faster. Don't you agree Patrick?"

Patrick looked at Aiden, then looked back to the chief and asked, "What does he call himself?"

"When we found him, he did not know his name. He showed us the initials and we did not know what to tell him. Then he said his name was Ian, so we call him by this name. Is this another name by which he is known?"

"Ian was our father's name," Patrick said. The chief nodded and listened more as Patrick continued, "At least he remembers something about himself, even if it is only our father's name. But Chief Sleeping Fox, we will take it from here and take him back among our own people. We thank you and do not hesitate to come to us if you need any more help."

The chief stood up and acknowledged the talk was over. They said their goodbyes and left the native's camp. Patrick told Aiden to head back to town and keep the operation going. He also told him to only tell James and Josie what was happening. As Patrick headed out to find Danny's camp, he had some worrying thoughts. He wondered if he would be able to get Danny to come back or remember who he was.

Patrick found Danny (now called Ian) and convinced him to go back to Yelm with him. Ian met many people and there were several ladies there and he fancied. He considered himself a 'ladies' man, so he tried his best to have good relationships with them. There was one lady who seemed to be a little shy with him, and he wanted to get to know her. He walked up to her and said, "Hello, my name is Ian. I think you're kind of cute, could you tell me your name?" Abby was shocked, she looked at Beth and didn't know what to say. Fortunately, Patrick had been watching Ian and came over to distract him.

"Ah! There you are Dan... ah Ian! I just found a job for you. Have you ever worked as a logger before?" Patrick said as he pulled Danny away from Abby and Beth.

"I'm not so sure I would have been able to keep my mouth shut," Abby said with a worried look for her friend.

"Abby, I'm not sure I wouldn't have said something either if Patrick hadn't come along. I don't know what to do about this. What if...what if Danny decides he likes me!? Oh Beth, I feel just awful, I can't do anything like that to you!" Abby was about to cry, and Beth was going to hug her when Dr. Lynne came by and saw them.

"What happened?" Dr. Lynne asked.

Abby and Beth both began to talk at once. When Dr. Lynne had it all sorted out, she said to them, "I wouldn't worry right now because he still isn't sure who he is. He will surely feel bad when he does remember if he starts courting Abby. So here is an idea. I know it is still too soon after losing Rusty, but could you get Max or one of the others to walk with you and make it look like you are taken? That may help him to look at Beth more." Abby nodded in agreement and said she would help. Both would make sure that Abby was not alone with Ian too much. They started to think of who a good suitor would be to play the role until Danny was Danny again.

CHAPTER 3

The days went on and Ian had procured work from Patrick and Aiden O'Donnell. He still didn't know what his last name was but now he had money in his pocket, and he could go courting. He was especially anxious to see the cute little lady with the brown hair and infectious laugh. Something was nagging at him though, and he still couldn't figure out what it was. He found out that he must have been a logger because he seemed to take to it easily. He also thought the men he worked with were being rather easy on him and that didn't make him happy.

At the end of the day, he cleaned up and went into the town hoping to see that one 'special' lady he was interested in when he first came got to town. He saw her and started to go toward her, when Aiden and a guy named Max grabbed his arms and took him over to the saloon. There he met Captain Sean, an older gentleman, who at one time had sailed the open seas. However, due to some health issues he quit the sea to 'sail' the open prairies.

"Well, They was right! You do look like me friend Danny, but what do ye call yerself now?" Sean asked.

"Well, I don't know about 'now,' but my name is Ian!"

The men talked awhile, then Josie stopped by their tables and said, "I do believe that it is almost time." Josie said with a wink to Sean.

"My dear Josie, I was just telling Dan...Ian here that there is a special lady he needs to meet, and I thought maybe you could go fetch her for him!" Sean said with a smile and a wink.

Josie wasn't sure his scheme was going to work but it might. She smiled back at him and said, "Sean, can you take your young friend here to the restaurant portion of our establishment and I will see if she is ready to come and visit with him?" Josie then left to call Beth.

"Well, my boy! Let's go to the restaurant and get ready for a fine supper!" Sean smiled and laughed to himself. Danny had a confused look on his face. He had no idea what Josie, the brothers, and Captain Sean had in mind for him.

"Shouldn't I be better dressed if we are going into the restaurant?" Danny asked as they went through the doorway.

"No, me boy, you are going to meet a young lady who has been waiting for some time now to meet you!" Captain Sean said as he saw some fresh meadow flowers sitting on a table. He grabbed them and handed them to Danny. "Here you go lad, just the thing to make a lady happy!"

When they got to the restaurant, Sean led Danny over to a quiet table with a view of Captain Sean's 'ship.' It was a prairie schooner he used when leading immigrants and others to various places out west. Danny had a bemused look on his face and was about to say something to Sean when he saw an angel, or at least what he thought was an angel coming toward him. All thoughts of Abby went out the window when he saw Beth. He stood up and smiled at her. Then he held her chair and helped her get seated. He was almost falling head over heels at first sight. He sat down and just stared at her. She was definitely not like Abby. She was a little taller and her eyes, oh those hazel/blue eyes. Beth thanked him as they sat. Dinner was served and a candle was lit. Patrick then had everyone step back to watch what happened.

"Hello, Miss. I don't think I caught your name."

"My name is Miss Sweeney," she hesitated for a moment then asked, "What is your name?"

"Ian Daniel O'Donnell at your service!"

Beth looked over at Patrick and wondered how she was going to help him come to know who he was. "Well, Ian O'Donnell, are you related to the O'Donnell's?"

Danny thought about it, then he said, "I don't rightly know. I think maybe, but those O'Donnell brothers seem to think my name is Danny!"

They sat for a while and ate their dinner, then Danny said, "Would you like to take a walk outside?"

"Yes," Beth replied.

After they finished their dessert, they strolled out of the restaurant toward a small sitting area outside. Josie had the loggers put the sitting area in. It had a small gazebo and a table with two chairs. She had plans to use it for weddings and other events. Ian walked next to Beth, being a gentleman as he always was, but then he stopped. The moon and the stars looked just right. He came a little closer to her and instead of asking if he could have a kiss, he immediately pulled her close to him and kissed her. He did so in a rather rough manner, so she pulled away and slapped him.

"What are you doing?!" Danny had never treated her this roughly and she wasn't sure that she wanted him to be that way.

"I thought you would like that. After all, they sent you in Abby's place when they knew very well, I wanted her."

Beth was furious and ran back to the hotel crying. When Sean and Patrick came out and saw Beth crying, as Karen was helping her back to the hotel, they went to find Danny. Patrick saw him and went up to him and asked what happened.

"Well, Mr. O'Donnell, that was the worst trick to pull on someone. You knew I didn't like that, Miss Sweeney! I want that other woman. And I don't need any help getting a woman, thank you very little!" He stomped off to the camp and didn't return.

CHAPTER 4

J acques Le Beau was just coming back to town
pulling a giant log that Mr. Smith had purchased
for him to work on. He planned to sculpt the log and
make into a fine statue for the town square. After
talking it over with Mr. Smith, he decided to create
a statue of the founding Fathers and Mothers. This
would include the O'Donnell's, Mr. Smith, and Josie.
Therefore, when he went to pick out the log, he asked
if Patrick would donate some wood for the statue
since it would include him and his brothers as well.

He opened the door to his artist workshop and
sat down. Pulling the huge log was exhausting work,
so he decided to make some coffee and have a little
something to eat. Beth was walking down the street
toward the mercantile when she noticed that Jacques
was starting something a new project. She wondered
what he was up to and decided to stop in to say hello.

"Hello, Mr. Le Beau!" Beth said as she stood outside
his door. Jacques turned around and was surprised it
was Miss Sweeney. He said hello and invited her in.

"I just stopped by to see what you will be creating for your next project." He seemed nice and she was in need of a male friend right now. She wondered if she should trust him.

"Well, if you don't want to come in, I can come outside. Would you like a coffee or tea?"

Beth nodded yes and then sat down on the chairs outside on the makeshift porch.

Jacques made some tea and brought it out to her, along with his coffee and a few biscuits to share. "Would you like some biscuits, Miss Sweeney?"

"Why thank, you, I think I am a little hungry. You can call me Beth."

"And you can call me Luis!"

"Why are you using your middle name?"

"Miss Sweeney, I mean Beth, I have found that my middle name is easier to pronounce and there are no hurt feelings if I use my middle name."

Beth thought about it and said, "Okay Luis, that sounds nice. What is your latest project that you are starting?"

"Well, Mr. Smith wanted a town statue in the square..."

"But we have the Totem Pole," Beth interjected.

"Ah, but see your Mr. Smith wants to be remembered, so he has commissioned me to create a statue. Now, in order to get the necessary materials, I need to go to the O'Donnell's and ask for a log from their mountain. Then I thought that Miss Josie should be included as well, since she is providing me sustenance for this project." He smiled as he finished talking about Miss Josie and Beth smiled too.

They had a nice conversation for a while, then Beth asked Luis if it would be okay for her to talk to him and get a man's point of view. He said of course and asked if it was possibly about the younger O'Donnell brother. She nodded yes and he said, "Let me get my materials, I will carve so I can listen to what you are saying." Beth was very impressed with his ability to carve and listen to her story. He came back and was ready to start on his log. "So, begin and do not leave anything out," he said and added, "even the intimate things, n'est-ce pas, No?" He smiled because he didn't want to really know any intimate details but was joking with her.

Beth didn't know much French, but she did know how to answer him in French, so she just said, "Those intimate things do not need to be told!"

Luis smiled and said, "Qui!" Then he nodded for her to begin.

"You know how we arrived. By train in Olympia, then we came to Yelm and lived in Josie's place for a while until some of us were married. The first social, the Reverend and Mr. Taylor, and a couple of others found their 'mail order' brides, the ones who answered their mail personally. I did not answer any mail but decided to come see if I could be a teacher and perhaps find a husband. I was interested in the dance, and while I was waiting to dance Danny O'Donnell stopped by with some punch, and we had a wonderful conversation. After that, I think we just started seeing more of each other and soon..." she started to cry a little and Jacques handed her his handkerchief.

"Oh, I am so sorry, I still am hurt!" she sighed and then continued, "He was the most innocent and honest boy that I had ever met. He was so shy, and he seemed to have a hard time forming words he wanted to say. He proposed to me once, and then something happened, and we didn't get married. We decided to wait a little while longer and had an 'understanding.' Then, a year later, my sister and brother arrived, and both my parents were gone. My other siblings took in the older ones, but the younger ones, well, I said I could take care of them out here. So, we put the wedding off another year. This was the year we were going to get married, but then the earthquake happened and well, Danny doesn't remember anything. I was very hurt when Captain Sean, Patrick, Aiden, and Josie tried to put together a romantic evening, thinking Danny would snap out of it and remember, but that didn't happen. And then when he treated me so roughly, I cried that night, and we haven't spoken since."

Luis was looking at his log and had started to work on a little spot when he stopped and looked at Beth, she was crying again. He went over and dried her eyes with his handkerchief. Patrick was walking by and saw them. He was about to go over, but he thought about events that happened in the past and didn't think it wouldn't be a good idea. Patrick continued walking but then decided to turn around because he needed to be sure there was nothing going on. He wondered if there might be something he could find out that would help his brother.

"Ah! Beth, I've been looking for you. I'm sorry about what happened a couple of days ago..."

"Patrick don't worry about it. I was hurt, but I'm okay."

"Patrick, what prompted you to stop by?" asked Luis.

Patrick looked at him with a little suspicion and replied, "Well, I just wanted to see how you are getting along with your sculpting."

"Oh, the log and I are just getting acquainted. Miss Sweeney stopped by to have a chat with me. She was curious about what this log was going to be."

"Well, Luis, I must be going, I'm needed at the hotel. Thank you for the tea and biscuits." Beth smiled at both Patrick and Luis and left for the hotel. Patrick said goodbye to Luis as well and hurried to catch up with Beth so he could talk to her.

Beth was halfway to the hotel when Patrick caught up with her and stopped her. At that same moment, Abby came running out of the hotel excited about something. "Oh, Beth, there you are! I have some important news to tell you!"

"I'm sure I don't know what it is. Are you going to tell me?"

"This is just too exciting! Excuse me Patrick, I need to see Beth in the most important way! Yes, Indeedy!" Abby took Beth's hand and walked her into the hotel. They went up to Beth's room and sat on the bed. This is when Abby broke the news.

"Beth, I think I have finally met the man I want to marry!"

"Abby, who is it?"

"He is a very nice man, he loves to eat and talk, and he is ever so gentle and kind!"

Beth looked at her and with her eyes she expressed some frustration because Abby was only telling her part of the story. Abby continued, "You know when Rusty died, I was just so devastated that I couldn't figure things out. Then I received a letter from my aunt who is not in the best of health, and she wants me to take care of her house until it is sold. She isn't doing very well. Anyway, I had a wire from a Mr. J. P. Featherington, Esq., who is my aunt's lawyer. He said I wouldn't need to go there to sell the house because he would like to come to visit with me to help me take care of her affairs."

"Abby, how do you know this man? If he has been taking care of your aunt's affairs, that is all the way back on the East coast!"

Abby looked at Beth with an exasperated look as if Beth should have known this and replied, "I thought you knew my aunt. Or was that your mother? Well anyway, Mr. J. P. Featherington is the son of Mr. Jack Paul Featherington who was my aunts' private lawyer until he passed. His son has taken over the business and has decided to bring his business here to Yelm!"

Beth looked astonished. She was happy for Abby but asked another question, "Is he single? How do you know his son?"

"We grew up together, Pete was my best friend. In fact, we played together when we were little, then his father sent him to a private school. We wrote letters but never really thought about each other. But he said in his recent letter that he wants to get to know me better. Doesn't that sound like he's interested in me?"

Beth bit her lip and thought very hard about what to say. She knew her friend Abby had trouble with getting a man. Sometimes it was her fault but most of the time the men she would meet, with the exception of Rusty, were not necessarily the best kind of men. There was one Beth remembered but he had to go to jail and make amends before he came back, and that was several years ago. "Abby, I hope this works out for you. Are you sure you are, okay? With Rusty being gone for only a few months I thought maybe you might need a little more time."

"A woman has got to get her man when the getting is good!" Abby explained. Beth could not help laughing about that. In fact, that was the first time Abby had seen Beth's eyes light up and heard her laugh. That was a good sign that Beth might be feeling better.

Just then, there was a knock on the door. Beth went to open it and it was Patrick. "May I come in?"

"I was just leaving!" Abby said as she made her way to the door.

"Abby, I need you to stay, there is something I have to tell Beth and I want you to hear it as well." Abby stepped back into the room and stood by Beth.

"What is it Mr. O'Donnell?" Beth inquired with emphasis on 'Mr. O'Donnell.'

"Beth, I can understand how you're feeling, with Danny not knowing who he is and all..."

"Mr. O'Donnell, you cannot possibly know or understand. To me, Danny has died. He is no longer. I do not even know if we can ever get back together even if he regains his memory! And if this is about my visiting Mr. Le Beau, well, that is none of your business. It is all innocent. What others say does not bother me. If it bothers you, well Sir, Danny and I are not engaged anymore, so it shouldn't concern you. What should concern you is how to help your brother. It seems that he has totally lost all comprehension of who or what he is!"

"But Beth, can't you hold on a little longer? Aiden and I are trying hard to help him remember."

"Mr. O'Donnell, I understand that you are hurting as well. And maybe your job right now is to help him remember, but after what happened a few nights ago, I do not want to see him anymore. Also, please tell him to leave Abby alone. She has a chance to meet someone she can marry, so if Danny stays away from her, she will get that chance. Now, good day Mr. O'Donnell and you no longer need to worry about me or Abby!"

Beth proceeded to push him out of the door and locked it. Abby stood there in shock as her best friend went over to the bed and laid down crying. She sat down next to Beth and held her while she silently prayed for her friend.

CHAPTER 5

Danny was up at the camp. He was very unhappy and very unpleasant to be around. The other loggers didn't want to be around him either, but Aiden came up to him to see what he could do about Danny's demeanor. "Hi, Danny, how's it going?" Ian didn't even look at Aiden. "I said, how's it going?" Aiden asked again but a bit louder.

"Are you talking to me? My name is not Danny, I am not an O'Donnell, my name is Ian, I'm still not sure the last name, and if it is the same, that doesn't mean I'm your brother!"

Aiden looked at his little brother and he was getting very upset. Dr. Lynne said this could go on for a year or two. He wasn't sure that he was going to last that long. Sometimes he wanted to slap Danny and shake him to 'wake' him up.

"Okay, okay, Ian. Hey, I thought you might like to take a trip to a cabin. It's near the lake and we can go fishing if you'd like?"

Danny looked at Aiden. He liked to fish. He wasn't sure if that was something he liked to do before, but he liked it now. "Okay, when do you want to go?"

"We have a few days off, so I thought we could go tomorrow and stay for about 3 days. There is some fishing gear up at the cabin. We can get a few more essentials and then we can be off." Aiden replied.

Danny decided it would be good to get out of the town for a little camping trip. He got up and went with Aiden to town to get the things they would need to go fishing. While they were in town, he saw Abby going to the mercantile to get some things. He was about to follow her when Aiden put his hand out and stopped him. Although he had not been able to talk to Patrick, they both decided to keep Danny from pursuing Abby.

"Hey!" Danny said, "Why are you stopping me? I want to say hello and apologize for the way I treated her!" He sounded like the old Danny, but Aiden was unsure.

Patrick had just heard the last of it and came up and stood in front of Ian like a tall tree that wouldn't budge and said, "Ian, do you think it is wise to pursue a woman who may be upset with you at this time?"

"Yes Ian, let her calm down a bit before you go. Besides, it's the woman who has to apologize to you." Aiden added. Patrick gave Aiden a funny look but let it slide. They had to keep Danny from Abby no matter what.

Danny looked at Patrick and Aiden and decided that going fishing would help clear his head. He had been having little headaches and wanted to be somewhere to clear his mind and think about things. "Okay, I think, I will wait. You are right, a man shouldn't have to apologize. Let's get ready to go fishing!" Danny smiled as they picked up some food and coffee for the trip.

Aiden told Patrick they were going to the cabin, hoping that Danny would remember something else. "Aiden, take him up to the tree where he spent the night with King, the dog we got him after father passed away. Do you remember where it was?" Patrick asked.

"Not quite, isn't it up by the old Hamby place? They moved many years ago, don't know if anyone is living there now."

"I think it will be all right. Just try it. Doctor Lynne says anything familiar might jog his memory. Maybe something from his childhood will be helpful. In fact, it was shortly after mother died when he began to stutter. Maybe that will help?"

As Aiden and Danny stepped out of their home with their fishing gear, Patrick was outside and Danny said, "I seem to remember something about fishing. There was something, but I can't quite put my finger on it just yet. Thank you, Aiden, for suggesting this trip. Is there a dog around here? I remember a dog." Danny started to rub his forehead. He was having some very powerful headaches lately. He didn't want to tell anyone because he thought the headaches were probably from a cold. Patrick and Aiden looked at each other with hope. However, they shook their heads and said they didn't have a dog in town. Patrick went to Josie's and Aiden and Danny got on their horses and rode to the cabin.

CHAPTER 6

It had been over a week since Aiden and Danny left for the cabin. Patrick went back to running the logging business, but he really didn't have the heart for it anymore. Abby and Mr. Featherington were now engaged and set to be married in June. Beth and Jacques L. Le Beau were getting along just fine, but Beth wouldn't let herself get too close to Jacques, even though he kept trying.

James Smith was coming out of his office at the mill and was headed over to Josie's when he saw Patrick on the street. "Patrick, how is Danny? Any sign that he might be recovering soon?" James asked, hoping that Patrick would be able to answer in the affirmative. He didn't consider himself a close friend of Patrick's, he was more of a business adversary, but the respect they had for each other was almost a friendship that went beyond the usual business deals. Patrick ignored James and didn't stop to talk to him. Then James followed him into the saloon where Josie was pouring drinks from behind the bar.

"Josie, your best, I need to talk to Patrick!" Patrick looked at James and was about to say that he didn't want to talk to him, then James gently shoved him into the back room as Josie gave James a drink and shut the door.

"Why did you do that James?" Patrick exclaimed, about to plow through him to leave.

"I know we don't get along well, but you helped me when I had the problem with Letitia, I want to return the favor!"

"And what are you going to get out of its James?" Patrick asked, realizing this may break him or make him stronger, either way James was ready to accept the challenge.

"Patrick, I know it's been over two years but if you recall we had a little bet."

"Yes, I recall that bet, what of it?"

"Well, since then we've been growing, and we are considered the 'Town Fathers' so to speak. But people are talking, and they are saying that maybe you are no longer the same O'Donnell who helped to start this town. They think maybe you don't even want to be a part of this town...." James let the sentence trail to give time for Patrick to respond. Patrick just stared at him. "Patrick, if you don't start pulling your share of work around here, you are going to lose customers and business. Not to mention, I may lose them as well since I am dependent on your loggers to keep my mill running, and I don't want that to happen!" Patrick just nodded again and took a sip of his beer.

James was planning to wait for Patrick to respond but he decided to say something else. "Patrick, if you can't get Danny back, I mean if he never remembers, you are going to have to let him go. He will be no good to you or anyone! In fact, I heard talk that some of your loggers want him to leave, because he's not pulling his own weight. And if Miss Sweeney thinks that he's going to marry her, I'm sure that is the furthest thing from his mind. You are going to have to cut the 'apron strings' Patrick O'Donnell, he is no longer a boy, he is a man!" James took a drink of his whisky and waited, hoping Patrick would snap out of the depression he was in.

There was a crash and splintering heard on the other side of the door in the saloon. Josie and her employee, Kevin Martin, went to the door to open it. "What in the H...is going on here? Patrick, why did you hit James? Why?" asked Josie. Patrick looked as if he was drunk, which he wasn't, he had barely had anything when James pushed him into the back room. Patrick sat down slowly. James sat down as well. Josie called someone to get a cold wet cloth to help clean the men up. While they sat there staring at each other, Kevin went back to the bar and someone else brought the cloths into Josie.

"All right, Patrick. Are you back to earth?" asked Josie as she stood between the two men sitting on the chairs facing each other. "I feel like Miss Etta should be here instead of me. You two schoolboys don't need to fight at a time like this!"

"Josie, I'm sorry. James, I'm sorry for hitting you. I just have no words to say about what's been happening to my brother. It seems as if we've tried everything, and nothing is working!" Patrick put his head in his hands.

"Patrick, if it's any consolation, I was trying to help you. I thought if I just goaded you, you might snap out of your own head and look at the situation in a different light." James explained.

"By attacking my family? Telling me I need to cut my brother loose from my 'apron strings'?!"

James looked at him sheepishly and said, "Yes. You have been chief cook and bottle washer and treated Danny as if he was still a child. You don't see that he has grown and become a man. Unfortunately, his memory is gone but that doesn't mean you should coddle him like an old lady! I thought that if I got you mad enough you would stop feeling sorry for yourself, stop seeing that this situation was your fault, which it is not, and that you would be able to help your brother. You failed the last try. That means you have to get up and try again! Where is the man with the fancy words who knows how to sweet talk anyone into doing something? Patrick, your brothers need you, the town needs you, and heavens, if you don't start using your head on your shoulders, you will lose the business, not just your portion, but your brother's as well!"

"What do you mean I would lose my business? Not to you!"

"No Patrick, but there is a logging corporation called Weyerhaeuser that has money and is willing to buy you out! Now, I don't mind if you get bought out, but I want you to be on top of your game and know what is happening. The way you have been, you have neglected some of your contracts, and some of your bills are piling up. YOU can't afford this Patrick! The town can't afford the loss of the lumber contracts as we are rebuilding and going forward with many projects." Patrick sat there stupefied, then he remembered that there was a businessman the other day who was asking about how they sent the lumber and who milled it.

James then added one more thing, "Patrick, one more thing, if you lose your logging business, you will lose everything you and your family have worked for!" James stopped for a second and then continued, "Patrick, there comes a time when as an older brother, you cannot shelter your siblings from life. Yes, Danny's accident has taken a toll on you and your family, but you cannot let this ruin you." "Josie, get us some fresh whisky, the private stock!" James called out to Josie. Patrick was taking this all in, he didn't stand up, nor did he make any move or sound. He just sat there. Josie brought the private stock in, and James poured it for him and Patrick.

CHAPTER 7

B eth and Abby were getting the list of things for the wedding when a knock on the door came. Michael came in and said that he had a note from Patrick O'Donnell. "Oh really, well I will look at it later. I think it might be an apology. Thank you, Michael."

"Uh...sis...he said I can't leave unless you read the letter." He waited patiently for her to read the letter and provide an answer. Beth looked at Michael and knew that Michael would stand there until he was told he could leave. He was learning to be a 'bellboy' for the hotel, and he already knew how to get the tips. She opened the note and was astonished at what she read.

"May I see?" Abby asked.

"I'm sorry Abby, but this is one letter I cannot show you." Abby looked unhappy but she wasn't for long. Sierra came in and said that Josie wanted to see Abby about the event planning for her wedding. So, Abby excused herself and left. Beth looked at Michael and

Sierra. Her brother and sister had grown so much in the few years since they had arrived there in Yelm.

"You can tell Mr. O'Donnell and Mr. Smith that I will be there tonight." Michael held out his hand for a tip and Beth looked at him like she did when he was trying to get away with something. She smiled and shook his hand, and he left.

There was another knock on the door, and it was Jacques. He had invited Beth to go on a picnic with him by the big rock near the lake. He definitely had plans. When she opened the door, she felt bad because she had to go see James and Patrick in a few minutes. "Oh, Luis. I am so sorry! I have an emergency. Could we step out about an hour from now?" Luis looked a little unhappy, but he was gracious and said, "No problem, Miss Beth. I can wait. The picnic can wait as well. Come find me at my workshop and we will go on a picnic then. Au revoir!" Jacques left and went back to his workshop to wait.

Patrick and James were waiting for Beth at his office at the mill. This was a very private office so there would be no one around to hear what they had to say. When Beth arrived, Patrick said, "Welcome Beth, may I apologize for the uncouth and disgusting way I have treated you?" He expressed himself with sincerity and humility.

"Why thank you, Patrick! I brought Sierra along to take down what was said in this meeting. I hope you don't mind." Beth replied as she looked at Sierra, who was writing everything down.

"No that is fine. Now, Miss Sweeney, Patrick and I have been talking and we would like to find another way to help Danny." James replied.

"Mr. Smith, I am through with Danny. You and Patrick can help him for all I care but since we are no longer engaged, and we no longer have ties to each other, I think that the O'Donnell's should take care of their own family and leave me out of it. The last time was too devastating for me!"

Beth was getting ready to leave but Patrick, again like a tree, stood in front of the door and said, "Now hear us out. Aiden and Danny are at the cabin. Aiden sent word that it seems like Danny is starting to remember and he sounds like his old self. But we need you to go take a trip up to the cabin and see if you can be of any help!"

"Patrick, that didn't work the first time, and I was very hurt by what happened. What makes you think it will work this time?"

"We were hoping that if we took you up to see him, he may remember who you really are."

"We tried that. I don't think that this idea will work!" Beth looked at Sierra to make sure she got everything written down.

"Miss Sweeney, we are hoping that he remembers more at the cabin." James said.

"What does Dr. Lynne say?"

"We haven't spoken to her for quite a while, but I think she would agree with us!"

Beth looked at both of them. She was still deeply in love with Danny and wished he would come out of this with his memory intact. "How much longer are they going to be at the cabin?"

"Aiden said he needed to get back to work, so he thought a day or two, unless you can stay with Danny while Aiden goes back to work?"

Beth looked at them and thought, 'stay with Danny, well that sure will start some gossip!' Then she thought how terribly lonely she was and how much she missed Danny. She did love him and now that she understood the consequences, or what she thought the consequences could be, she agreed. "Okay, I will do that! But only on with the understanding that if this does not work, or even if it does, we may not be able to get back together. But for Danny, I will do this!" She nodded and Sierra finished writing down the exact wording. James and Patrick were happy.

"Beth, thank you!" Patrick said appreciatively and asked, "Could we leave tomorrow morning?" She looked at him and said, "Yes."

Aiden was still up at the cabin. Danny had seen pictures of their father and mother. He thought that he was Ian, since he felt he resembled him. He began asking where his wife was? Aiden said she was visiting some family. He had been saying that for a week now. He was ready to give up, but Patrick got word that Beth would show up soon. Hopefully, this would help Danny.

Not only did Danny think he was Ian, but he also thought his wife was Enya, and she was still alive. When Beth arrived, Danny said, "Well, there is my darling Enya, come home!" He was so welcoming. He made her sit in a chair and then started to talk all about what was happening out with the trees and such. "Well, Enya me darlin' how are you? You are just about due to have that babe, any day now dearie!" Beth sat there, in shock. She knew they weren't married, and that she definitely was not pregnant, but she had to play along a little to see if this would help.

"Well, my dear Dan—Ian, how are you? I missed you so much. What with visiting our closest friends and all. The baby is fine, he will be a fine lad when he is born!" She smiled a lot and pretended. Danny was also a lot nicer than he was back in Yelm.

"I will get the bed ready, and we can go to sleep soon. You are a welcome sight, my love!" When it was time for them to go to bed, Beth made up some excuse about why she couldn't sleep with him. He was willing, since he thought she was far along in her pregnancy.

CHAPTER 8

Danny woke up and realized Beth was in the other room. He went to her and touched her tenderly. She acknowledged his touch; it was a gentle loving touch. She stood up to start the fire and make coffee. Surprised that he had already started the fire, she smiled at him, and he smiled back. This felt normal. She went to the bedroom to change and then came back out to start making the biscuits. Danny had gone out the door for a shave and as she was making the biscuits, she looked at the original pictures on the mantel. She thought she could almost recognize Enya's picture, although it seemed to have faded by now. It was after all about 40 years old and those tin-types didn't last very long. After stoking the fire and setting the biscuits near the fire, she went to the table. There was a diary there and she opened it up. It was Enya's diary. She wondered why she hadn't seen it the night before.

"Well, dear, how did you sleep? I know that we have a fair bit of work to do, clearing the land and whatnot, but a kiss for the morning won't be too bad now, will it?" Danny asked as he reached down and bestowed a gentle kiss on her forehead. "Where are the boys? They should be sitting at the table by now. No, don't worry, I will call them. They are probably outside." Danny went to the door and opened it. He walked outside but didn't find them. He was perplexed and he was sure he had spoken to Aiden the day before. He forgot who was in the cabin and why he was there and walked on down to the meadow near the cabin. It was a cold day. Well, to him it felt like winter was coming on, or maybe it was the spring, he wasn't sure. He didn't see the trees or the forest but kept on walking just the same.

Beth was in the cabin wondering where Danny had gone. He had walked outside and hadn't come back. She was worried that he had gotten lost, so she went outside and called him. "Dan...Ian!" she called out the door. She didn't see him, so she put on her shoes and went out the door. The wind was getting a little stronger. Thankfully, she wrapped her coat around her and went in the direction of the meadow.

The skies grew dark and all of a sudden, a down-pour came. Beth lost her footing and tumbled down the side of a hill. Danny was within earshot and heard her scream. He looked around and didn't see anyone, but he saw a shadow. He followed the shadow and came to the hill. He looked down and saw her laying on the ground in the mud, water was rushing towards her. He knew immediately that she was in a gorge that would fill up with water and she would drown. He didn't remember her but the shadow that was near him urged him on.

He climbed down the hill and saw the rushing water coming toward her, fast and furious. He got down and grabbed her. She was soaked but easy to pick up. He got her to the other side, which wasn't so much of a hill as the other one. In fact, he was able to walk up the little hill carrying her. He looked for some kind of shelter and saw a hollow in a tree. He made his way there with her in his arms. He placed her gently in the hollow and he saw that there was room for him as well. He snuggled up beside her and fell asleep.

It seemed like it was a long time before the rain stopped. When it did, Danny woke briefly and thought he saw his mother standing nearby with King, his dog. He wanted to get up, but she shook her head no. He fell asleep again. Beth was sleeping as well. When Danny woke again, the sun was shining and he felt dry, he thought that was curious but hastily checked on Beth. "B-B-Beth" he said. Then he crawled out of the tree and looked around. He seemed to be waking up from a dream. "Beth!" He said again, but she was unresponsive. He decided to make a small travois to carry her back to the cabin. He didn't question why he knew he was near the cabin, but it seemed to him that he was near there.

Beth stirred a little and he took her hand to see if she was okay. She had a raging fever and he wondered how he would get her home and to the doctor. He wished he had a horse to help get her safely to the cabin or into town. But he didn't see a horse. 'It probably ran off when the rain started,' he thought as he created a soft mat out of the branches that were on the ground. Then he pulled two long poles and using his knife he cut the extra branches off. It took quite a while. Finally, when he was finished, he gently picked up Beth and placed her on the mat. Then went to the front and picked up the poles and proceeded to find a way down the hill they were on. He was familiar with the terrain, so he took her the way of least resistance. He stumbled once or twice because he himself hadn't been feeling well either.

He heard a whinny from a horse a little way to the north. He found a safe spot to leave Beth and decided to check out the horse he heard. "Beth, Beth, my love, my dearest, I will be back for you. I heard a horse whinny. Perhaps I will be able to get us a ride." He looked at her and she looked so peaceful sleeping. "I will be back!" Danny said with determination in his voice.

The horse was still making its noise and he hurried toward it. When he got there, he saw what was happening. The horse was stuck in a stand of trees and couldn't get out. The halter was stuck, and Danny didn't know how long it had been there. He quietly came up to the horse and whispered in its ear. The horse quieted down and he was able to loosen it from the trees. He checked the horse's hooves and was satisfied that it wasn't lame. It was a hard task to have to shoot a horse that was lame, and he was glad he didn't have to do it! He slowly walked the horse to where Beth was laying. He picked up the small trees he had torn from the ground to make the travois and attached them to the horse with what was left of the rope and saddle.

Patrick and Aiden had arrived at the cabin, and it had been two days since the storm came through. They wanted to go check on Danny and Beth to see what was happening. Aiden saw something and called for Patrick to come take to look. "Looks like the horses are gone but there is no telling which way they went or if anyone was on them!" said Aiden, as Patrick came out of the cabin. Both men stood there thinking of what they could do. Not long after, an Indian on his horse was coming toward them. When he got closer, they recognized him as Chief Sleeping Fox. "Patrick, come, your brother has found himself and his woman, they are by the river." They followed the chief to where Danny and Beth were. "Patrick, Aiden! Thank goodness you are here! Beth is very sick. She fell in a gorge during the rainstorm, and I pulled her out. I remembered, I remembered!" Danny exclaimed as he held Beth in his arms.

PART 3
WOUNDED HEARTS/
HEALED SOULS

CHAPTER 1

Beth was heading to visit Jacques Le Beau when Danny came up to her. It had been several weeks since he had seen her last. She was better physically, but emotionally she still felt like she had lost something. She didn't understand what it was, but when she saw him, Danny, coming toward her, her heart clamped shut and she just nodded as she passed by. She would be respectful and cool, but she could not, or would not open her heart to him again.

Danny on the other hand, recovered nicely from his bought with amnesia and felt that everything would be all right. He felt that he and Beth could still work through this, and they would still be in love like before. But try as he might, he could not get Beth to stop and listen to him or even say much more than a polite word or two.

"Good day, Mr. O'Donnell!" Beth said curtly walking by him.

"Good Day Miss Sweeney! How are you doing today?"

"I am doing quite well today, thank you. And How are you, Mr. O'Donnell?"

"Quite well!" he said with the thought that 'at least she is talking to me.' Then he said, "Miss Sweeney, I would like to know if you would go on a picnic w-w-with me next Sunday?" Beth thought for a moment because they had gone together before the earthquake. She wondered if this was a good thing or not. "Mr. O'Donnell, may I let you know tomorrow afternoon?"

"It is fine. You can call me Danny," he said nervously, and all of a sudden, he was shy about taking her on a picnic.

"Thank you, Mr. O'Donnell! I need to go now," Beth said as she walked away. She had no idea why she told him she would let him know tomorrow. She would have to talk to Josie or Nancy about it later that day. Danny stood in the middle of the street and breathed a sigh of relief. He was happy that she at least talked to him. He decided to go to the saloon and have a drink and see if Aiden or Patrick were there. He needed to talk to them about what to do next.

Beth entered Jacque's workroom. He was still working on the statue for the town square with Mr. Smith and the O'Donnell's. As he stood there looking at his 'masterpiece,' Beth knocked on the door. "Ah! Miss Beth, it is good to see you today. How have you been? I am puzzling this problem out. Would you like to take a walk with me? I have some bread and cheese and fruit and a little wine."

"Oh, thank you, no Jacques, I mean Luis. Besides, I don't drink. But if I can help you with your problem I will try!" she immediately went over to the carving and looked at it. "It is beautiful! But I don't see anything wrong with it."

Jacques came up behind her and gently put his arm around her waist. "Oui! It is beautiful but it is missing something, I cannot say what it is, but it is surely missing something," Jacques explained.

He turned her around and looked at her. She was beautiful, and more so with the light streaming through his workshop window. He then gathered her up in his arms and was about to kiss her when she pulled back. He looked shocked, and so did she. "What is it, Beth?" Jacques asked, hesitant to do anything else lest he frighten her away. Beth looked confused and shocked. She was unsure of what she was feeling at the moment. She looked like a deer about to run.

"I-I-I... don't know," she said in a trembling voice. She was trembling all over and he could see that. As he gently put his arms around her again.

"Beth, it is okay, it is me Luis, your friend and confidant, perhaps lover?"

She pulled away from him again and with a little scream, she ran out of the door. He stood there in shock and then decided to take a walk by himself to think about what had just happened. He was a little confused. Was it because she had been confiding in him so much that he felt this way? Was it because he hadn't had the love of a woman for so long that he was in need? He took his bread, cheese, and wine and went out toward the nearby lake to fish and to think.

Nancy, the minister's wife, was just about to go out of her home when she saw Beth running aimlessly through town and she went over and stopped her. "Beth! Beth! What happened?" Nancy shouted when she caught up with her. All Beth could do was sob. Nancy took her inside and sat her down in the parlor. She made her some tea and soon Beth had quieted down enough so Nancy could talk to her. "Oh, my Beth, I am so sorry!" said Nancy, who at that moment was about 6 months pregnant and had no idea how to help her friend.

"I don't know Nancy. I just don't know. Maybe I can ask Josie to see what she has to say." Beth said as she dried her eyes and drank a little tea.

There was a knock on the door and Nancy went to answer it. "Nancy is Beth here?" Danny asked as he stood outside the door. "I was heading to the mercantile when I saw Beth running down the street. Is she okay?"

"I'm not sure what happened but when she is ready to tell you, or anyone else, she will let you know."

Nancy replied as she shut the door. Danny felt a little uneasy, usually when Beth was upset, she would talk to him. He couldn't remember how he treated her nor what he said when he had amnesia. Nancy went back to the parlor and told Beth that Danny saw her running and crying, and he was concerned about her.

"Thank you, Nancy, for not letting him come in. I'm not sure I could handle talking to him right now." Beth said as she sipped her tea.

"Are you ready for my news now?"

"Yes" Beth said smiling and almost back to her old self.

"Peter and I are going to have a baby!" Nancy said with a big smile and a glint in her eyes. Beth was overjoyed. This was the best news she had heard all day. She hugged her friend and then the continued to talk some more. When Josie arrived, Beth was laughing and happy again.

CHAPTER 2

In his shop, Jacques was carving and putting some finishing touches on a couple of the statues he made. He had the O'Donnell brothers, James Smith, and Josie. He wanted to carve Beth as well, but now, with the confusion of feelings, he couldn't bring himself to do that. He couldn't figure out why she ran from him when he tried to kiss her. He was still confused and wanted to call on her to find out what exactly her intentions or thoughts were about a relationship with him. Maybe she was just his 'muse'? 'No, it cannot be, I have never felt this way about a 'muse' before!' Jacques thought. His muses were just short bursts of lust and as an artist he knew all about that.

Standing there in front of his statue, Jacques concluded that he should find out what she wanted, and who she wanted. He put his tools down and put on his jacket. He walked to the hotel and brought some wildflowers he picked on the way over. When he got to her door, he knocked hoping that she would be there. There was no answer. Just as he was about to knock again, Beth came around the corner with some towels and other necessities for the rooms. "Oh, hello Jacques!"

"Hello, so now I am Jacques? You no longer call me Luis?"

"Let me put these in the storage room and I will be with you in a moment." Beth said while looking around for one of the other girls who worked in the hotel. She would have liked her sister, Sierra, or Josie to be with her. She opened the storage room door and put the items on the shelf. As she was beginning to close the door, Jacques cornered her.

"Ah, Miss Beth, we need to talk. I have missed you so much." Jacques said as he was bending down to kiss her. She tried to push him away and was unable to do that. Just at that moment, Danny walked up the stairs and saw what was happening.

"Beth!" he shouted. Then he turned and ran down the stairs, hurt and saddened by what he saw. At that moment, she found the strength to shove Jacques away from her and run after Danny. It was too late, he was gone! She stood at the top of the stairs as Jacques walked up to her.

"I now know what you have decided. Go to him, I will not stand in your way. Please do not stay with me, as you have played with my affections for too long! NO! Good day Miss Sweeney. Do not come to my studio again!" Jacques fumed out of the hotel and walked quickly back to his workroom.

Beth stood still, trying to cry but not able to. She didn't know what to do. Josie came around the corner, saw her, and took her to her room. After she got her to sit down on the bed, Josie made some tea and they sat quietly for some time, then Josie asked, "Beth, what happened?"

"I-I-I don't really know. One minute I was putting the linens on the shelves, the next minute Jacques cornered me and tried to kiss me, then Danny saw me and thought that I and Jacques....OH, oh, oh...."

Josie sat for a moment and thought, then said, "Beth, remember I told you that you have to bend with the wind and be flexible. Well, this is more serious than that! You have been seeing Mr. Le Beau alone for a while now. Ever since Danny wasn't himself and said those awful things to you. You have been courting Mr. Le Beau. Mr. Le Beau naturally thought you were interested in him, but I don't think you were. You, Beth, were just using him because Danny hurt you!" Josie knew those were harsh words for Beth to hear but she had to hear it from someone who loved her like a daughter. Beth sat on the bed crying and sobbing. She heard what Josie said and knew it was true.

"Beth, you need to talk to both of these men. Unless you confront this, you will have no peace within. You need to come to an understanding with them and yourself or you will not be happy!" Josie said as she stood up. "I need to go take care of the saloon. Let me know if you need me to be with you when you do confront them. Remember, Danny is no longer a boy, and you are no longer a girl. You are a woman, and as such you need to be a woman and stand up for yourself and those you love!" Josie explained as left the room and shut the door.

Danny was walking along the water and thinking to himself, 'Why is she doing this to me? What did I do to her? I only want to love her and care for her?' Patrick came up to him and said, "Danny, we need to get back to the camp, there is work that only you can do!" Danny looked at Patrick and shook his head yes. He thought that maybe if he threw himself into work, he could forget her and never look back. But what if, he thought, 'what if he had to see her? What if she remained in Yelm. He couldn't marry her now. She had been with someone else! That is, it!' thought Danny, 'I will get Patrick to send me to Olympia and start a new office there. I am good at selling. My honesty and integrity will help me there. I will talk to Patrick later. I need to think on this.'

By the time they got back to camp, Danny was doing better on the outside. Patrick looked at him but said nothing. He knew what happened. Josie had gotten word to him about Beth. All he could do now was wait for Danny to want to talk about it, then he might be able to help. Mr. Le Beau finally had an answer now and he was going to see Mr. Smith to tell him he needed a vacation before he could finish his statue. He decided to leave for a month, but the statue should be finished by July so they could still have a big celebration. He was cleaning up his tools when Patrick walked in to ask him something.

"Mr. O'Donnell, how are you?" Jacques said.

"Well, I've been better. I want to know what happened with Miss Sweeney today. It seems she had a problem?"

"Sir, that is not between you and I, perhaps your brother and I, but not you. And I certainly will not talk about what happened with you!"

"I realize that what happened between you and Miss Sweeney is confidential, but I want to know if you have been courting her?" Patrick inquired. Jacques looked at him in amazement. No Gentleman would ask such a thing unless it were another lover! Perhaps Patrick has been in love with her as well, he thought.

"Mr. O'Donnell, since you are the oldest, I will tell you. I did not start courting her. In fact, she came to me shortly after her little spat with your brother. She has been coming to visit quite often. Up until today (he did not tell Patrick about what happened a few days ago) I thought she had an interest in me. But

I am a simple artist and for a young lady, a young gentlewoman, to take interest is something which I cannot express how grateful I feel. However, when I made advances to her, she resisted and would not respond to my advances. Your brother saw that, and I should tell you she is playing with you. She has no intention of loving anyone! So, if I were you Sir, I would send her away from here and then you will be at peace with yourself, and your family will be at peace. For, there is no peace when a woman has been scorned or cut to the heart like hers has been. She is trying to find her way but not at my expense nor should it be at yours either!"

Patrick listened to what Mr. Le Beau said, taking it all in, then he said to Jacques, "Thank you for telling me. I heard you will be leaving soon. Will that be for good?"

"No, I need to finish the statue for the town. I will return in a month or two. However, if that woman crossed my path, I shall step aside and avoid her evil ways forever. A man cannot live with a woman of that sort in the same town. She could cause havoc with his life and never regret it! Good day Mr. O'Donnell!" Jacques said as he turned his back on Patrick.

Patrick stood there for a moment, then nodded and left. He had some thinking to do. He had to talk to Danny and make sure he was okay, but most of all he had to talk to Beth. She seemed to be the most honest and true woman, and the best choice for Danny. But maybe, just maybe what happened between them a month or so ago, might make it too hard for them to find their way back to each other. Patrick had to try, Josie did as well.

As Patrick left the workshop, he saw James coming toward him walking rapidly and very upset. "Hello, James, we need to talk sometime..." Patrick said as James flew toward him.

"Yes, yes, sometime. I need to see that artist. Is he in his workshop?"

"Yes, I just left him, that is what we need to talk about!" Patrick said loudly as James pushed past him and stepped into the workshop. Patrick shrugged his shoulders. He figured he would talk to James later. While Patrick was walking away, he heard a shout and a gunshot coming from the workshop and he raced back immediately.

CHAPTER 3

Barney was closer than Patrick and got to the workshop first. What he saw made him laugh. James was standing behind the statue and had a look of fear in his eyes. Jacques was standing with a gun pointed, not at James, but at the statue. He shot all 5 bullets into the statue and the worst damage was where Danny and Beth's likenesses were. "I tell you now, Mr. Smith, I will not be back to finish this statue, nor will I return or tell anyone else to return to this place. Only when I have finished destroying my statue and this building, I will leave!" said Jacques furiously.

"You will not destroy my building. You owe me rent!" Barney exclaimed after he heard Jacques talk about destroying the building. He told Jacques that under no circumstances would he allow the destruction of his building.

"So be it! I will not destroy the building, but I will take my materials and destroy the statue! Mr. Smith, you will pay me half since I did work on the statute for the last month!"

James looked at Jacques and being the businessman he was, he said, "No! Mr. Le Beau, you did not finish your contract. I will pay you ¼ of what was left of your commission. That should get you out of Yelm and far enough away that you will not have to show up here again!"

"Monsieur, Oui! That is acceptable. I expect it in time to leave for the stagecoach unless the train is leaving sooner. I do not wish to spend another day in this town!" Jacques was not happy to say the least. Barney proceeded to inform him that neither the train nor the stagecoach were due until the next Tuesday. James gave him what he was owed, then Jacques looked around at everyone, and they all left. would not spend another night there. He arrived walking in, and he would walk out. That afternoon he cleared his things, grabbed his tools and some food for the trip, and left on foot vowing never to return.

Patrick and James sat at the saloon and talked about everything that happened. "James, I don't suppose you could help with Beth and Danny, could you?"

"O'Donnell, I don't understand you. You're asking for my help with Beth and Danny? I think those two need to talk to each other! Why on earth, you know the last time I helped with Beth and Danny was a disaster! Not only did Danny break Beth's heart, but he also showed his true colors. I might also add if it hadn't been for you, Josie, and Nancy all ganging up on me, I think they would have worked it out quite well on their own!" Patrick looked at James in shock. He didn't know why James would insult Danny like that.

"James, why would you insult Danny by saying he 'showed his true colors?!' I take umbrage at that and want to know what you mean?"

"Well, O'Donnell, ..." James began and then very carefully said the following, "I have known you for a very long time. You and your family are very close, and I admire that. However, sometimes when help is needed, it is wiser to stay out of the situation rather then get involved. What Danny said to Beth that night is unforgivable, and I don't blame Beth for looking somewhere else. After all, she and Danny have been together for the past several years and they have not gotten married. You have a lot on your hands. I think that you should stay away from Beth and Danny and don't involve yourself any more than you have to. Also, don't let your other brother get involved either. Danny will calm down and Beth will calm down as long as everyone, and I mean everyone, stays out of the picture."

At that moment, Edith and Edna, the Crumple sisters, walked in. Patrick and James saw them, and they both knew that those two were always gossiping about something. James looked slyly at them and said, "With those two, we might have problems. I think I will send them on a little tour of the northwest." Patrick knew it would be a good idea to keep those two from gossiping. The fuel for the fire would die out and both Beth and Danny might get back together on their own.

"What are you suggesting James? Tie them up and throw them in the water?" Patrick said jokingly. He was ready for some mischief anyway.

"Oh, nothing like that. There is a tour of the Pacific Northwest by train coming in and it's heading back to the east for the World's Fair. I thought they could use a nice 'vacation.' I will pay of course, but if you will help convince them they need to go, I think it might work? After all, no fuel, no fire!"

Just as Edna and Edith came up to their table, Patrick nodded to James in complete agreement. "Ladies, how are you? Please sit down, would you like a soda or a cup of tea?" Patrick asked. They agreed, and Patrick went to get their drinks, which gave James's time to explain the 'vacation' to them.

"So, Ladies, would you like to take a trip to the World's Fair by train? I would pay your way and provide you with spending money as well. A private car and of course you would bring back some souvenirs. We could highlight the World's Fair here in our own brand-new museum! Who knows, we might hold the

World's Fair in our city some day!" Patrick returned with the drinks and sat down.

"Oh, but James, we would be traveling alone would we not? I do not think it would be appropriate for us to be alone on such a trip!" Edith said.

"Oh, goodness no, is there someone who could accompany us?" Edna asked.

Patrick and James looked at each other. Just then Beth walked in from the restaurant side of the hotel and Danny walked in from the front of the saloon. "Hello, Mr. O'Donnell!" Beth said to Danny. "Hello, Miss Sweeney!" The tension was so thick you could cut it with a knife.

Patrick suddenly had an idea. The ladies could be the chaperones. He excused himself and asked James to follow him. "Oh, you can't be thinking that can you, O'Donnell?" James asked with surprise.

"Why not? Beth and Danny need to be alone and away from everyone in order to find themselves again. Perhaps with these ladies as chaperones it will be for the best. It could happen!"

"Patrick, how will you get Danny and Beth to go on this trip with each other, as well as those two gossipers?"

"You know, I never told you how Danny stopped being so shy. It was when he discovered Beth. She was nice to him, and she didn't demand anything from him. They were honest with each other. Neither of them had been hurt before. So, that 6 months was sort of a precourtship. Why can't this be another one? They will have the best chaperones money can buy and they can get to know each other again!"

Josie came up and asked what they were talking about. When she found out she agreed with Patrick, and said, "Those two need to get back together, otherwise they will both be miserable. It is a good idea for Edna and Edith too because they will have fun as well." Josie saw that she was needed at the concierge desk and left. James looked at Patrick and nodded his head in approval. He couldn't figure out how Patrick had cautioned him to stay away from them, and now he was involved again.

"Ladies, as you know, Danny and Beth have been having problems. We would like you to be chaperones on this trip. You will be asked to help Danny and Beth as well. What do you say?" The ladies looked at both men, then looked at each other and said yes simultaneously. They would take a trip on the train, then come back again. Maybe those two "children" would get back together again, but if not, they would have found what they needed either way.

"You are going to have to foot the bill for Beth and Danny!" James said to Patrick, who just smiled. "One more thing, Patrick. How are we going to convince Danny and Beth to go along with this plan?"

"Leave that up to me James. I will get those two on the train together." Then Patrick left the room to find Aiden.

CHAPTER 4

Patrick knocked on Beth's door. When she opened it, she saw it was Patrick, "Oh, it is you! I have nothing to say to you! Good Day Mr. O'Donnell!" Beth was about to slam the door closed when Patrick placed his foot in the doorway.

"Miss Sweeney, I do believe that Edna and Edith would like to talk to you for a moment." As he stepped aside, Edna and Edith came up to the door.

"Oh, please come in Miss Edna and Miss Edith!" Beth said in surprise and immediately pulled up two more chairs. Patrick was about to come in, but Beth looked at the ladies and who both shook their heads no. So, Patrick left, and Beth offered the ladies some tea and biscuits.

Patrick went directly to Danny and asked if he would mind going on a little trip with the ladies. He would look after them and help them with their luggage, connections, and other various things that a man should do for a lady. He didn't tell Danny that Beth would be going along as well. The next day both

Beth and Danny showed up in front of Josie's Saloon and Hotel. They were surprised to see that each of them had been 'hired' to help with the ladies. "Mr. O'Donnell, I hear that we will be traveling companions with the ladies. Just what is your job to be? Mine is to assist the ladies as a traveling companion and nurse if needed." Beth said coldly.

"Well, Miss Sweeney, mine is to assist the ladies with their luggage and transportation!" He smiled and didn't tell Beth what the plan was. Patrick told him it was a way for them to get back together after all they had been through, and Danny was hoping he would be able to get reacquainted with Beth during the trip.

Beth stared at him for a moment. She was a well brought up young lady, so she didn't feel the need to respond to his comment, but she wondered why he had smiled. It looked like there was a twinkle in his eye. 'What had Mr. O'Donnell told his brother?' she thought as she climbed into the wagon.

The ride to Tacoma was comfortable. Beth sat with Edna, and Danny sat next to Edith. Patrick was driving the wagon along with Aiden, who was going along because they had some important business to do in Tacoma. The Northern Pacific Railroad had arrived as far as Tacoma, and although Yelm tried to get it to go farther, there was an economic downturn, which essentially stopped the progress of the railroad to Yelm. The prominent Judge in Yelm was Judge

Thomas Burke, whom Nancy's husband worked with in the legal department. Not only was he a judge and lawyer, he also was the one who tried to have the Railroad President, James J. Hill, bring the railroad to Yelm. It was still quite a few years before there would be a railroad terminal in Yelm though. So, the O'Donnell's, along with Miss Sweeney and the sisters, traveled by wagon to Tacoma from Yelm. It would take most of the day and they had arranged to stay the night in a nearby hotel to catch the train heading East.

"Oh, Miss Edna, this is such a beautiful day for a ride in the wagon, isn't it?" Beth said, trying to have a pleasant conversation. Patrick told her that she needed to go with the sisters to help them and be a companion for them while they traveled. Edna agreed and asked Beth about what her future plans were. Beth didn't speculate, nor did she give any hint as to what she was planning to do when she returned. "Well Miss Edna, I'm not sure really. I do have the job at Josie's hotel. I suppose I will go back there when we are finished with our excursion." Beth said as politely as she could.

"Well, my dear, what about your young gentleman?" Miss Edna asked. Before Beth could answer, Patrick, who had overheard the conversation, interrupted the conversation to point out the scenic view of the Nisqually River flowing through

Yelm. He expounded on the clearness of the river and how they had fished there many times. By the time he had finished his 'lesson' on the flora and fauna of the river area, both Beth and Edna had forgotten what the question was.

They had finally reached Tacoma and stopped in front of the Hotel. Aiden would stay overnight with the ladies and Danny, while Patrick left to get back as soon as possible to continue work in the camp. After settling in, Miss Edna and Miss Edith were both in the same suite as Beth. Aiden and Danny were in another room. "Aiden, why do you suppose he wants me to go along with them, why can't you?" Danny asked.

"What did Patrick tell you Danny?" Aiden asked as he stretched out on the bed reading a logger's magazine. Danny thought for a while.

"He just told me to remember some of the things I did while I was not myself, and then he quoted Shakespeare. Something about a razor wounding a heart!"

"Well, there you have it. Ponder on that line. I think he was thinking of something that happened between you and Beth that might have a bearing on what he told you." After a while, Aiden said, "Danny, I think I will take a nap for a while. Been up way to early today and I feel tired. Check on the ladies. Isn't that what Patrick said was your job? To take care of the ladies and be sure they aren't harmed or bothered?"

Danny stood at the door and decided to take a walk around the town. They had a reservation for dinner downstairs, and he was expected to escort them to the dinner. He thought about what his brothers had said and why he was picked to do this. He wanted to leave and start an office in Tacoma or even Olympia. He really didn't want to renew his relationship with Beth. Not at this point anyway.

'Well,' he thought, 'Maybe I will do a little research and see how people would take to having a lumber company with an office in Tacoma or Olympia. As Danny was walking to the park, he saw Beth walking toward the park as well. She had taken the afternoon to walk and take in the sights. He was unsure of going over to see her, but he remembered he was there to take care of all the ladies, including Beth. So, stayed back but followed her to be sure he could protect her. At least he thought so.

Danny was so intent on following Beth that he didn't realize she had turned down the wrong ally. He went back a few blocks looking for her. He tried not to panic as he walked back checking every alleyway he could. 'Where did she go?' he thought. Now he was very worried. He turned down an ally and heard something. Cautiously, he waited, and heard a scream. This time he recognized that scream. It was Beth! He ran toward the scream and saw a couple of burly men grabbing her and trying to drag her somewhere. He ran up to them and was able to get one swing in when the other man knocked him out. Beth saw him and started to cry. They held her and covered her mouth. She bit him and ran to help Danny. The men looked at her, not saying anything. They laughed and grabbed her and took her with them.

Aiden was just waking from his nap when there was a knock on the door. He went to answer it and it was Miss Edith. "Oh, Mr. O'Donnell, where is Danny? Where is Beth? They were supposed to be here, and it is almost supper time?" Miss Edith said with a worried look on her face. Aiden looked at the time on his watch.

"Don't worry Miss Edith, I will go look for them. I will walk you to the dining room and then I will go look for them." After taking Miss Edith and Miss Edna to the dining room, Aiden left the hotel and went to search for Danny and Beth. He looked down an alley and he noticed someone moving around a bit. It was Danny who was just waking up from the beating he received. When Danny saw his brother, he said, "Aiden, we have to find Beth! Do you know where they may have taken her?"

Aiden looked at Danny and replied, "Do you remember where they took us last time?" Danny remembered when he and Aiden had almost been shanghaied there in Tacoma.

Danny nodded and they went to find Beth. As they went down the alley, they heard another commotion.

Beth was standing at the end of the ally with a gun pointed at the men and one woman. "Don't come any closer, or I will shoot!" Beth yelled. The men looked at one another and then went toward her. She had her hand on the trigger, and suddenly the gun went off. Beth fell backwards and the men backed away. One of them had blood coming from his shoulder and the woman shouted, "Let's get out of here!" They took off running, however, because of the gunshot the police had been called. Both the police and the brothers arrived at the same time.

Aiden and Danny ran to Beth. "Beth, Beth are you okay?" Danny asked as he helped her up.

"Yes, Yes, I am, thank you Danny."

The police came over and told them they apprehended another set of 'crimpers.' Beth was relieved that Danny and Aiden had found her, but suddenly she fainted and fell into Danny's arms. The police told them to come down to the station and pick up the reward money. They said they would but wanted to wait until Beth felt better.

"I think I better get you back to the hotel room so you can freshen up." Danny said to Beth kindly.

"I will pick up the reward Danny. You take Beth back and get cleaned up for dinner tonight." Aiden said as he brushed off his pants and started to walk to the police station. Danny looked at Beth and asked her if she was okay. He asked if she wanted to take his arm because she was still a bit unsteady. At first, Beth wasn't going to, but she still felt a little faint, so she did. It seemed so very natural.

When they got back to the hotel, Beth went to the room with the Edith and Edna, and Danny went to his own room to clean up. Aiden arrived a bit later and told them they received 10,000 dollars for the reward, and he deposited it into their bank account.

"Aiden, did you keep Beth's reward money out?" asked Danny.

"No, I put it all in so we would be safe, and they would be safe. I will make sure she gets it when you two return, or you can get it out if you need it for this vacation you are taking."

"Well, I think she would like to at least have it nearby. I know she doesn't have a bank account but maybe she can keep it in ours."

Aiden cleaned up and they headed to the lady's hotel room to escort them down to dinner. While they were eating, Beth asked Aiden and Danny about the reward money. Danny told her that Aiden put the money in the O'Donnell account, but if she wanted to have it, she could get it any time.

"Mr. O'Donnell, I am not sure I like you making decisions for me. I remember distinctly you are telling me that you did not like me to say that you would do something without consulting you first! So, why did you not consult me first?!" Beth said to Aiden in a very stern, but polite voice. Danny looked at her and at Aiden and thought to himself, 'This was going to be a long trip.'

"Beth, Aiden was just thinking that since we are away from home, the less money we carry the better because we don't want to have anything stolen. He was trying to keep you and the other ladies safe." She knew he was right. They were better off having it in the bank, but she wanted to let him know that she would like to be consulted first, especially when it came to finances.

"Thank you, Aiden and Danny, for looking out for us," Edith said to prevent any further disagreements. "My Beth, you and Danny sure did have some excitement today! This will be a very exciting trip with the two of you together!" Edith looked to Edna for agreement. The ladies were happy and felt the company they were in should be happy too. For Danny, he was just wondering what he had gotten into. But for Beth, she so dearly wanted to get back together with Danny. She still had to curb her reactions and stop and think first before speaking. Josie was right, she ran right to Mr. Le Beau. Truly, she had hoped that Danny would be jealous seeing her with another man, but that was not the case. He had amnesia and wasn't the same Danny as before. Beth did feel sorry about how she used Mr. Le Beau and she wanted to apologize again, but that wouldn't happen.

After dinner, the brothers went back to their room across the hall and Aiden asked, "Are you doing okay Danny?" He was concerned for his brother, especially after the fight he had in the alley.

"I am fine, thanks Aiden. I know that I hit my head a little, but it seems to have knocked some sense into me."

"Why did you say that, Danny?"

"I did a lot of thinking about what Patrick told me about my actions when I was not quite myself, and how Beth was very hurt. It explains a lot about why she has been overly polite and not willing to share with me like she used to." Aiden waited for a minute and was about to say something when Danny continued, "Aiden, I think I still love her. It hurts and yet, when I am around her, I feel...feel more alive. I feel like we were meant to be together, to be married!"

Listening to his little brother and knowing him as well as he did, Aiden knew that eventually they would soften and open up to each other. Aiden said, "Danny, do you remember when you changed your mind about marrying Beth because the other guys talked you out of marrying her?"

Danny thought for a moment then replied, "Yes, I do, and I remember you asking me what brothers are for and I said to pick up the pieces."

"That's right little brother. Now I know Patrick thought this trip might help you and Beth find your way back, but we also want you to know that if it doesn't work out, we are still here to 'help pick up the pieces!"

CHAPTER 5

Abby was busy fussing around her little domi-
cile when Sierra came in with a telegram for
her. It was for both of them from Beth. "Aunt Abby,
Aunt Abby!" Sierra called from the foyer. Abby came
to the foyer.

"What is it, Sierra?"

"A telegram from Beth!"

"Oh, my! It is addressed to all of us! Is
Michael around?"

"I think I know where he is, I will be right back!"
Sierra ran out of the door and over to Sean's 'ship.' It
was really a large raft used to ferry people, animals,
and wagons across the Nisqually river. Michael was
learning the how to tie knots like a sailor, and Sean
was working on the raft that was used to transport
people and things across the Nisqually river. "Michael
Sweeney!" Michael looked up when he heard Sierra
calling him. He hoped it wasn't something he had
to do for her or Abby, he wanted to be a sailor and

then a captain, like Sean. Well, like him when he was younger anyway.

"Over here Sierra, what's up?" Michael asked as he finished tying a bow knot.

"We have a telegram from Beth! Aunt Abby is going to read it. It is addressed to all three of us! Hurry!" Sierra shouted as she ran back to Abby's house. Michael called to Sean and said he would be back soon. Sean said okay and Michael was off. When he got to Abby's house, he was winded.

"Oh my, do you want a glass of water Michael?" Abby asked. He shook his head yes and drank the water. Then they all sat in the parlor waiting for Abby to read the telegram.

"Okay children, here goes...

Have made it halfway to ST Paul, STOP.

Will be traveling again tomorrow STOP

I am sending letters to each one of you STOP

Love Beth STOP!

"Well, that was brief. When the mail gets here, we will all have letters, won't that be exciting?!" Abby said with excitement. Michael and Sierra looked at each other and asked,

"Aunt Abby, why didn't she say more? Do you suppose that her and Danny have patched things up and are going to get married there?"

"There isn't much room for a lot of small talk in those telegrams and it is awfully expensive. I am sure she kept it short for that reason. She is sending each of us letters and we will get them in a few days or so, I think. It will depend on if the mail is on time or if Sean is getting the mail!" Abby giggled at that little joke she made and so did the children. They knew sometimes Sean would bring the mail from Tacoma and sometimes it would arrive by stage.

Michael and Sierra were glad to hear that their sister sounded okay. They missed her and worried about her because of all she had gone through. A few days had gone by. Sean left the day after the telegram arrived and was not expected to return for about a week. The O'Donnell's ran their camp okay without Danny, and James was doing well with his business. Since Abby had married a lawyer who was part of Judge Hill's office, they were invited to a special party. It was a 'fundraiser' for a railroad terminal to be built in Yelm. They hoped that eventually the trains would get to Yelm in the next year or so.

Patrick was checking the books and making sure the bids and contracts were in line, when he received a letter from Danny. He looked at it and was about to open it when he saw that it was addressed to both him and Aiden. It was still too early to call a lunch break, but he decided to wait until after work when he and Aiden were at home and could read and discuss what was happening. James entered the tent just then and Patrick put the letter away in his pocket. "Hello, Patrick, have you heard anything from Danny yet?"

"No, I have not. Why do you ask?"

"Oh, no reason, I just wondered if they have patched things up and were ready to get married."

"Okay James, what are you thinking?"

"Oh, nothing really, but this trip is costing quite a bit for us. If Beth and Danny don't get married, or at least come home engaged, I think I will have to take at least his third of the mountain since there is only one bride left and she is, shall I say, 'unmarriageable'?"

Patrick was just about to belt James in the mouth when Aiden came in. Aiden heard only the last little bit and was just as upset with James, as Patrick was.

"James, she is not unmarriageable, and they will patch up their differences and you will not gain even a square foot of this mountain!"

"You know James, I know you want Mt Tahoma, but I'm sorry even I can't make that decision alone without Danny! So, you can leave before one of us becomes unrestrained!"

Trying to cut the tension, James interrupted and said, "Well, that is good! The O'Donnell brothers are back to normal. Now, I can get back to what we really need and that is more lumber for the railroad ties and tracks that Judge Hill will pay us to build. There is a meeting tonight in the event room at the hotel and you and your brother are invited. However, if you feel you can't be civil, I will have to ask you to leave. We will be voting on some issues about who will be providing what for this project and I thought you might like to be in on it!"

Patrick realized that once again, instead of a despicable enemy, he was an honest businessman and respected the O'Donnell's, but he also wanted to make money as well.

"Okay, James, what time is this meeting?"

"It will be after the fundraising dinner Mr. Featherington has planned to garner support for the railroad. Did you not get an invitation?"

"Yes, yes, we did. However, the cost is a little too steep for us at the moment since we are paying for Danny and Beth's trip." Patrick explained.

"Yes, I understand it might be steep, but it might be worth it to get to know some of the benefactors of this project. Maybe you could go by yourself and leave Aiden at home?"

"James, that is none of your business! Thank you for informing us. We will be there tonight! Good day James!" Patrick replied sternly as he looked at Aiden and they left the tent. James was left standing alone for a minute but walked out of the tent to is carriage and headed back to town.

Chapter 6

There was an important businessman from Yelm on the train. He and his wife were also one of the first passengers traveling to Chicago for the fair. Danny wandered out of their car and was walking through the dining car, when he noticed Mr. Blaine sitting with his wife eating a light lunch. "Hello, Mr. Blaine, Mrs. Blaine" Danny said as he was walking by.

"Hello Danny, why don't you sit with us for a while?" Mr. Blaine requested.

"Oh, okay" said Danny, surprised that Mr. Blaine knew who he was.

"Your brother, Patrick, is doing well with his logging camp. Does he have any ideas on growing his business?"

"Well, he does have ideas, but you would have to talk to him about them." Mr. Blaine looked at him thoughtfully.

"Danny, why are you on this train? Are you perhaps scouting for another investor?" Mr. Blaine took a bite of his sandwich and Mrs. Blaine was eating her soup and listening as the men talked.

"W-w-well, no that is not right. I am escorting Miss Edna and Miss Edith to the World's Fair." Mrs. Blaine perked up and asked, "Is Miss Sweeney with you?"

"Yes, she is. Would you like to visit with her? I can go back and get her?"

"No, that won't be necessary. Besides, I would enjoy visiting with all the ladies. I think I will go there myself and leave you two to talk 'business.'" Mrs. Blaine stood up and excused herself.

Both Mr. Blaine and Danny stood up and waited until she left, then they continued their conversation. Meanwhile Mrs. Blaine stopped to talk to the waiters and asked for some tea and sandwiches be brought to the car that Mr. O'Donnell was in.

Mrs. Blaine arrived at the car door and knocked. Beth opened the door thinking it was Danny but was surprised to find a lovely woman standing at the door. "Hello, may I help you?" Beth asked thinking the woman was lost.

"Oh, no Miss Sweeney, I am here to help you!" Mrs. Blaine said as she walked in, and the tea cart followed. "Ladies, Miss Edna, Miss Edith, how are you?" Edna and Edith were very excited to see Mrs. Blaine. They helped on the Ladies Auxiliary with her and were delighted to see her again.

"Minerva, how are you? You are looking well," Edna said.

"Minerva darling it is a pleasure to see you. We didn't know you were on the train, otherwise we would have sought you out and had tea with you!" Edith added.

Mrs. Blaine laughed and said, "I didn't know I was going until the last minute when Edward said we were going to the World's Fair this year and going on the first transcontinental train I might add!"

Beth stood politely nearby and Mrs. Blaine, after receiving affectionate greetings from Edna and Edith, turned to Beth, and said, "Miss Sweeney, I am Minerva Blaine, head of the Ladies Auxiliary and Society for the beautification of our fair city of Yelm."

"Hello, you can call me Beth!" The ladies sat together and had tea. They talked about the city of Yelm and what improvements could be made to attract more people to come live there. Danny returned with Mr. Blaine who said hello to everyone, then he and his wife left to their respective car and turned in for the night.

"Beth, I don't mind that you and your young gentleman sit up and talk but I do believe you should say goodbye to him shortly," Edna said, then Edith continued, "We do have a busy day tomorrow. We will arrive at St. Paul, and I do believe we have another train to catch to Chicago. So why don't you stay for half an hour more Mr. O'Donnell, and then leave." Danny and Beth agreed, especially since the ladies were retiring and Beth did feel a little tired as well.

The next morning, they had to change trains and Danny made sure their baggage was already on the next train and that the ladies were there as well. They sat at the train station waiting for the train to Chicago. Mr. and Mrs. Blaine were with them since Mr. Blaine decided to talk to Danny more about logging and expansion of the logging and ranching business. He was interested in James' point of view as well, but Danny said he did not know what James' thoughts were.

Edith and Edna were talking with Mrs. Blaine about flower gardens and museums, and of course other interests that would make Yelm a special place to visit or live in. Beth decided to take a walk along the platform. She was quite happy deep in her thoughts. She sat down and took out her journal and wrote the following:

> "Well, we are almost to Chicago! We will
> be there sometime tomorrow and then
> the next day we will be at the fair. My
> thoughts have been very mixed. Danny
> is back to being his sweet, honest self,
> and I cannot help but feel an emotion
> that has been missing since before

the earthquake. I wonder if he feels the same way. We talked a little but did not have time to get too deep. He was polite and wanted to say more but I think he is worried that I may not react positively to what he will say. I so much want to say I am sorry, and I don't know how to bring myself to that. I know that he hurt me, but I also hurt him. How will we come together? Will we be the same as before? Oh, I pray that he and I will be together soon!"

Beth

She looked at what she had written and decided that it was enough! What more could she say? The letters she sent to her friends back in Yelm were friendly, although she did not confide too much, especially to Abby who would let everyone know what she said. But then again, Abby seemed to be more thoughtful now that she was with child. Perhaps having a child will calm her down some. Anyway, Beth noticed the train had arrived and headed back to the platform.

Danny was frantically searching for her. He wanted to find her and make sure she was all right. He thought she had been hurt or worse because of the last time when she took a walk in Tacoma. When he saw her stepping back on the platform, he breathed a sigh of relief. How he wished they could really have a conversation with each other. The night before had been too formal. She was polite but reserved and he was just being a gentleman letting her lead the conversation. He wanted her, but she didn't know. What was that stanza from Shakespeare his brother Patrick had taught him? 'How do I love thee?'

"Mr. O'Donnell?" Beth said as she came up to him. He stopped his musings and said, "Oh, there you are! Are you ready, we need to get to the train, they are boarding right now. The ladies are already in the car." He took her arm to guide her to the train, and Beth let him. That was more than she would have let him do before. Although she thought of herself as an independent woman, there were times when she felt it was better to compromise in little things rather than start an argument. She figured this out early on but still had her moments. Especially when she felt strongly about a subject, such as women voting! The train started to roll out of the station as Beth and Danny hurried onto it. They missed their train car and had to walk back about three cars. They were walking back when the train yanked forward and backward, and Beth fell into Danny's arms.

CHAPTER 7

J ames was walking back to his office when Barney
came with a telegram for him. "Thanks Barney!"
he said as he took the telegram. Barney then ran to
the logging camp to give Patrick his telegram.

"Is Patrick here?" Barney asked.

"No, he's up supervising some of the trees. May I
help you?" Aiden asked.

"This is for Patrick. When he gets back can you tell
him to come to the mercantile?" Aiden agreed and
Barney slowly walked back to town. He was thinking he
would have to get someone to help with delivering the
messages. Maybe he could have Michael help out. He
could pay him 10 cents for every delivery. He decided
he would ask him when he saw him next. When Barney
got back to his store there was another surprise. Abby
was in his store looking through catalogues.

"Oh, Hello Barney, I was wondering if I could order
some baby things, please. I have decided I am going to
have a boy! So, I will need to order all blue!" Abby said.

"I will be back in a moment," Barney said as he went to the back room to look for his notebook to take Abby's order.

Barney's wife, Emma, was in the store as well and replied, "Abby, how do you know it won't be a girl?"

"Because my aunt says that if you carry high it's a boy, and if you carry low it's a girl, or is it the other way around?"

Emma laughed. "That is toward the end of the pregnancy Abby. Not at this point. Have you felt the quickening?"

"No, what is 'the quickening'?" Apparently, even though she helped others through the birthing process, she hadn't really paid attention to what happens during the pregnancy.

Emma continued to explain, "It happens about the 5th month. It's when you feel the baby move, kick, or something like that."

"I don't think Dr. Lynne told me about that yet, Emma. I will have to ask her when I see her next week. She wants me to come in every week for a checkup. I don't really understand why, but she is the doctor, yes indeedy, she is the doctor! Oh! Here comes Barney."

When Barney returned, he gave Emma a peck on the cheek. He went around the counter and asked Abby what she wanted to order. "I think I will have to wait until I see the doctor. Good day Emma, Barney."

Abby said as she walked out of the store and went to her husband's law office to visit with him.

Barney looked at Emma with a puzzled look on his face. "I'm sorry Barney, she was going to buy baby things and wanted blue. She was sure she was going to have a boy, but I talked her out of blue. Then she, being Abby, was a little confused so she must have changed her mind, at least for now."

"That's okay Emma. She will be back. We know Abby well enough by now!" Barney said with a smile and a chuckle.

James got back to his office and looked at the telegram. It was from Mr. Blaine. He wanted to meet with James and the O'Donnell brothers when he got back from his trip. Patrick burst into the office and was fuming. "James, I thought we worked together, why is Blaine sending me this message to meet with you and him when he returns?"

"Patrick, I don't quite know. That is what I got in my telegram as well. He didn't let me know we were supposed to meet together at the same time. I suppose yours has more information?" Patrick took a second look at his telegram, then he read it a little more closely.

"It says here that he and Danny have met and had some conversations about expanding the logging and milling operations here in Yelm! Do you suppose that Mr. Blaine and Danny have met at the World's Fair?"

"Well, that could be. Have you received any messages or letters from Danny concerning that?" Patrick looked up and thought about it for a minute, then said no he hadn't. Both James and Patrick wondered what Danny knew.

"Patrick, can you send a telegram to Danny asking him to clarify things for us? By now he's at the hotel and I'm sure they will give him the message." He needed more information before he agreed to a meeting with Mr. Blaine. As for Patrick, if Mr. Blaine wanted to talk to both of them, Patrick would need to know more as well.

"Yes, I will get to Barney's right away and send the message." James stood up to say goodbye because he too was heading out of his office to see to something on the milling floor that Jack had asked about.

Barney was taking care of a customer when Michael walked in. He was helping Sean fix the raft, and also was getting some supplies for Captain Sean to use when he traveled to Yelm by boat from Tacoma. "Michael, just the man I want to see!" said Barney. Michael smiled shyly when Barney called him a man, he was only 12 but he perked up when anyone treated him like an adult. "Would you like to make a little extra money? I have a job for you."

"What do you want me to do?" asked Michael.

"I need someone to take telegrams to people in and out of town. I will pay you 10 cents for every delivery and 15 cents for out-of-town deliveries of telegrams!" explained Barney as finished up with Captain Sean's order.

Michael looked at him and decided that would be a great idea. His sister told him he was still not old enough to go with Captain Sean. When Sean left, he would have nothing to do except go to school and hang out with the other kids. He liked to work and earning a little money always helped. "Yes, Barney, I think that would be fine!" Michael said with all the confidence of a 12-year-old who thinks he is already a young man!

"Good. I will need you here at the store daily between 6 and 8. You can go to school, then come back after school and wait for messages. Sometimes the messages will already be ready for you to deliver. I may have supplies, which if you can find a horse, you can use that to deliver supplies to the outlying areas as well."

Just then, Patrick walked in. "Hello, Patrick, how are you?" asked Michael.

"I'm fine and how are you?"

"I just got me a job!" Michael shouted.

"Well, that is good, doing what?" Since Beth and Danny were gone, Beth entrusted Michael's well-being to Patrick.

"I'm going to help deliver telegrams and supplies for Barney and he's going to pay me for it! But I need a horse. Do you have a horse I can use?" Michael asked.

Patrick stopped and thought about it, then asked Barney, "Barney, why would Michael need a horse to deliver telegrams?"

"I thought I might extend his job by having him deliver supplies to the outlying farms."

"How many supplies are you talking about? Wouldn't he be better off with a wagon?"

"I didn't think of that. You know, I suppose it would be better!"

"Do you have your delivery wagon? If he's going to make deliveries, he could use that, and a horse for those other things as well!"

Barney agreed and Michael was ready to start work that day. Patrick stopped Michael and asked, "How are you going to go to school and do your homework?"

"I'm helping Captain Sean right now. When he leaves, I will do my homework after school while I'm waiting to deliver, and I can also do it after I'm done with the deliveries. It's only a couple of hours."

"Since your sister has put me in charge, as long as you do your homework and keep your grades up you can do this, but if you start having problems then you will have to stop. Is that understood?" Michael agreed as he took the supplies for Captain Sean and walked out of the store whistling and happy.

Patrick smiled watching him leave. 'He is going to be a fine young man some day!' he thought to himself. Then he turned his attention to Barney. "I would like to send a telegram to Danny." Barney went over to his telegraph office and got ready to write down the information.

The Blaine's, Danny, and the ladies found they had rooms in the same hotel. They all had reservations at the Palmer hotel and were happy to find the accommodations were excellent. The ladies had a suite on the second floor with a room across the hall from Danny. The Blaine's suite was further down on the same floor, and a bit larger of course. Danny opened the doors to the ladies' suite, which had a sitting room, three private bedrooms, and a washroom. The bellboy brought up the suitcases and trunks and set them in the appropriate rooms. Danny paid him a tip and stood there watching as the ladies hurried to their rooms. He wanted to say something to Beth, but she had already gone to her room.

"Beth, Miss Sweeney?" Beth heard her name and came out of her room.

"Yes, Mr. O'Donnell, Danny?"

"I just wanted you to know that I am across the hall if you need me." He said with a quiet shy smile. The same smile he had when they first met all that time ago. She looked at him and almost smiled but keeping her propriety.

"Thank you, Mr. O'Donnell, Danny!"

"You are welcome, Miss Sweeney, Beth." They both laughed and said good night. Danny left the room and walked to his room where he sat on his bed and smiled at the thought. Maybe, just maybe they could patch things up.

Danny began reading the information about the fair. He was determined to find a way to get Beth alone. He looked at the rides and something called a 'Ferris wheel.' He thought that would be a nice start. Then he saw information about the night they would be lighting the electrical pavilion and he thought 'that is it!' He still had the ring he was going to give her when he was supposed to propose to her the first time. This time he could propose to her in the lights. He laid down on the bed and thought, 'If she says yes, will she be willing to find a minister and get married legally?' He fell asleep dreaming of that thought.

Beth laid on her bed. She desperately wanted to be with Danny. She didn't understand why, after all this time, they hadn't been able to talk about their feelings. How was she going to get him alone to talk to him? She had to accompany the ladies to all the exhibitions they were going to see, but she had to talk to him. She had to make things right, and if he still wanted to, if he asked her this time, she would say yes without hesitation and would even marry him there if they could do it. They could have a real wedding when they got back to town. Beth fell asleep dreaming of Danny as well.

Chapter 8

S ean arrived with mail for almost everyone in Yelm. When he was finished with unloading, he carried the mail to Josie, Barney, Abby, Aiden, Patrick, James, Michael, and Sierra. Everyone received two letters. The first letter was sent by Danny and Beth while stopping in Montana, the second was more personal and also carried some valuable information for James and Patrick. It was a sight to see; everyone stopped to read their letters. This gave them all something to talk about, especially Abby. Beth wrote to Abby but was very careful not to say too much. She wrote to Patrick as well. Patrick and Josie were the only ones to receive three letters each. What she had to say to Patrick and Josie echoed Danny's letter to Patrick. He didn't write to Josie, but he told Patrick he could discuss things with Josie when they returned.

The whole town was quiet for about an hour. Josie's saloon sat silent, no one wanted to disrespect those who were reading the letters, since letters were usually few and far between. A couple of trappers came into Josie's and waited for a while until she finished her letter and was able to serve them. Even trappers knew how valuable a letter was, since most of them never received any, except maybe at Christmastime from family members if they had any.

Michael was the first to finish. He was excited because Beth was going to bring home some treats. He never had gum before or Cracker Jacks! Sierra was excited as well because Edna and Edith found a special doll just for her and they were going to bring it back with them.

James, Patrick, and Josie planned to have a meeting later that evening. Danny told them he met Mr. Blaine, and that Mr. Blain was interested in developing property and other business projects. Barney was excited and telegraphed Danny to ask if he would bring back some pancake flour and a couple of the other snacks and foods that he heard about from the World's Fair.

Abby was too excited to think. Yes, she would try the pancakes, and of course if Beth would send her the Perambulator (a fancy stroller for her baby), she would be very happy. Edna and Edith also wrote to James thanking him for the train ride and said they would bring back a souvenir as well.

Later that day, James, Patrick, and Josie sat together in James' office to discuss the situation with Danny and Beth, as well as the improvements that

Mr. Blaine was hoping to create when he returned. "Patrick, do you think we have enough lumber for these projects? I would have to hire more men." James said, as he sat at his desk with Patrick and Josie sitting beside each other. "I think the O'Donnell brothers will be opening offices in Olympia and Tacoma to handle some more areas of logging and I'm going to send Aiden out that way. There are a couple of towns that may provide workers for these projects as well. We are going to have to hire more workers. In fact, you may have to branch out as well!" Patrick said firmly.

James thought about it and replied, "I will check with Jack to see what we can do. Maybe I can hire someone to open a new mill out that way so that we can mill your logs." Josie interjected and asked, "James, Patrick, did you forget why this trip was formed? It wasn't necessarily formed to improve Yelm, although that is not a bad idea! The main point of this was to get Danny and Beth back together, and from what Beth has said to me, it might be working. They are on speaking terms. Edna and Edith wrote to me and said they seem to be getting closer and closer every day. They said they would be going to the fair and once they are done for the day, they will leave them alone to discover each other!"

Both Patrick and James listened to Josie. She was right, this was for Danny and Beth. It seemed to be working. They were on a mini vacation and from what Danny had told Patrick, it was working! "Josie, what did Beth say that makes you think she is softening?" asked Patrick. James' interest was piqued as well and as Josie was about to answer, Abby burst in and wanted to tell them something.

"Oh, I just have to tell you I received my letter from Beth, and she sounds so much better than she has in a long time. Thank you, James, for sending her on this trip!" Abby said excitedly. James acknowledged her gratefulness and both he and Patrick waited to see if Abby had anything more to say.

"Abby was there anything else?" asked Josie.

"Hmm? Oh! Why yes indeed. Beth says we are going to have a women's auxiliary when she returns, and Mrs. Blaine will be leading it! She said the Blaine's have been in contact with the Olmstead brothers, you know them? They are the ones who designed Central Park in New York! Well, they are coming to design a few parks here in Washington and Beth says that I will be with them on the Board! Isn't that wonderful?!" Abby exclaimed loudly because she couldn't contain her excitement.

"Yes, I think that will be great, she also said that to me in her letter as well Abby!" Josie replied.

"Oh, it will be wonderful to have a beautiful park to walk in on a nice afternoon or maybe evening." Abby said as she was thinking of strolling through the park with her new baby in the perambulator. Josie saw that James and Patrick needed to talk more about the business side of things, so she excused herself and ushered Nancy out the door. Patrick and James were thankful that Josie could distract Abby. They wanted to talk more about the improvements and knowing there would be a park in Yelm, was something Danny had forgotten to tell them about.

"It seems as if our fair city is going to prosper, along with Danny, Beth, and the O'Donnell brothers, and of course you too James!" Patrick said with a smile. James smiled back and said he would get Jack there and Patrick would have Aiden there as well.

Barney was so delighted he was going to have new merchandise in his mercantile. The ladies would be coming in to purchase this 'Aunt Jemima's' pancake flour and perhaps the loggers would use it as well. Business was going to be booming. Emma came in with their son and daughter to tell Barney about the plans Beth had for the Beautification of Yelm and that she too would be on the Board of the Ladies Auxiliary.

"Sierra, when will Beth return?" Michael asked.

"Oh, I think they will be back by next week. Why do you ask?"

"I want to try the new gum but most of all I miss her. There are some things a little brother needs to talk to his older sister about!" Michael explained.

"I'm your older sister too, Michael!"

"I know, but I mean a grown-up older sister!" He turned around and went to Barney's to see if he had any deliveries for him.

Sierra stood there feeling upset because her little brother wouldn't confide in her. As she was standing there, Aiden came around the corner and saw her. "Hey Sierra, what's got you so down? Didn't you get a letter from Beth?"

"Yes, it's just that Michael wants to talk to Beth rather than me! We have always been close, but he wants her instead of me! Sometimes I wish I didn't have an older sister!" Sierra said stamping her feet and looking miserable. Aiden looked at her and sat down on a bench nearby. He motioned for her to come sit by him.

"You know Sierra, I am a middle child. I have one older brother and one younger brother. Sometimes, Danny would rather talk to Patrick than me about things. He and I were close in age, and I always thought he would confide in me rather than Patrick. But that is not how it happened. You see, even though you are closer to Michael in age, it doesn't necessarily mean that he will always confide in you. He will have certain things that maybe your older sister can help him with that you can't. It doesn't mean he has stopped confiding in you. It just means that there are some things he will tell you and some things he will tell Beth. And just between you and me, he may not even tell either of you because he may have problems that Danny can help him with."

Sierra looked at Danny while she thought about what he said. She knew instinctively that he was right and also that being a girl, she wouldn't know what to answer if he asked her something boys knew that girls didn't. Then she wondered about something Aiden had just said, and she asked, "I understand that now, but I have another question." Aiden looked at her to indicate that he was listening, and she continued, "Do you think Beth and Danny are getting back together?" Aiden realized she was putting things together and he didn't want to give away what the trip had been all about, but at the same time he didn't want to lie.

"I think you would have to ask Patrick." Aiden said goodbye to Sierra and went on his way. Sierra sat on the bench for a little while, then went to Abby's to help her.

CHAPTER 9

Danny escorted the ladies to the Children's Building. This was the creation of Bertha Palmer and her Board of Lady Managers. They sought contributors for this from authors and poets, such as: Rudyard Kipling, Oliver Wendall Homes, as well as the President of the United States, Benjamin Harrison, and Tchaikovsky, who contributed a seven-bar manuscript composed in 1871 as the second movement of his string quartet No. 1. All of this was for a children's book to help contribute to the "Children's Home of the World's Columbian Exposition, which was published by Hayes and company in 1893. The ladies were excited about this and purchased one book for the library and one for Beth.

They stopped at the beer garden and had 'hot dogs' or Vienna sausages as they were called. Danny had a beer and the ladies had soda. Edna said to Edith, "You know, it's about time we left these two to themselves."

"Do you suppose it's all right? I mean, aren't we chaperones after all?"

"Yes, of course, but we have known these two for a long time. If they were going to do something they shouldn't do, don't you think they would have done it already?"

Edna and Edith had begun to soften up towards Danny and Beth, whose marriage to each other had been thwarted for so long. Edna sincerely wanted them to get married and start a family. She liked Beth, and if she had a girl, she would have wanted one like Beth. Edith looked at Edna and knew that whatever she would say, Edna had made up her mind.

"We would like to return to our hotel to get a little rest before this evening. Edith and I want you two to go and enjoy the evening together without two old ladies hampering you!" Edna said. Beth looked at Danny, and Danny looked at Beth, they tried not to smile but both were thinking the same thing.

"I will escort you ladies back to the hotel and take our souvenirs with us so we can put them in the room until later. Beth, would you mind waiting for me at the music pavilion?" Danny asked.

"Yes, I will meet you there. Are you ladies going to come back to see the electrical exposition?"

Edith looked at Edna, and Edna looked at Edith, then Edith said, "I think we will see it tomorrow night, you two enjoy the rest of your day. We will see you tomorrow. Beth, do you have your key?" Beth said yes and Danny escorted the ladies to their hotel room.

Beth was listening to some of the beautiful classical music when Danny got back. Being the gentleman that he was, Danny came up to the table and asked if the seat next to Beth was taken. Beth smiled and said no. They sat at the table for a while and when the piece was finished, Danny stood up and helped Beth up as well. They went outside and he said, "How daring is you?"

"What do you mean?"

"I hear there is a ride that we can take where we can see the whole world from the sky." Beth hadn't really had a chance to read the literature about the Ferris Wheel, but it did look like a lot of fun so she replied, "Okay, I think we can try it!" Danny's heart almost skipped a beat. 'Was this going to work?' he thought. He took her hand, and they walked over to the Midway Plaisance Pavilion and looked at the Ferris wheel. It was getting a little late, but they still got in line and waited.

Beth picked up the information about the Ferris wheel and exclaimed, "Well, well! It takes us up about 240 feet! And the cars hold 40 people!" She looked up and wondered how she would like it.

"That isn't very high. The trees back in Yelm are higher than that!" He thought back to one of the first times he was allowed to top a tree. Patrick didn't like the idea, but he was the only one that was able to handle it. Beth thought about being on a very high cliff as she watched the waves crash on the rocks when her family had visited the coast of New England.

Beth gave a little shudder, then Danny put his arm on her shoulder, and she smiled and calmed down. "It says here the ride is about 30 minutes and we get two revolutions per ride," Danny continued. Beth and Danny moved up the line and were finally getting ready to enter the next car that stopped. The conductor on the car called out 'all aboard' and they filed in with a few other people. Danny found a space at the end with the window so that they could look out and see everything, while he played with the ring in his pocket.

The car started slowly, and after about three more cars filled up, they were moving. It stopped at the top so Beth and Danny could look out of the window, then it came down. They were both fascinated by what they saw. When it came to the top again, it stopped and that is when Danny pulled out the ring and knelt on one knee to ask Beth to marry him. Beth was so surprised that this was happening. She thought she was in heaven. This time her answer was yes, and he put the ring on her finger as he gently held her close, and she cried with joy.

"Yes!" she said loudly, and she was surprised that she actually said yes. Danny was in heaven himself. When the ride was over, they both floated off and went down to the pavilion. They sat for a while without talking. "Danny" Beth said. "Beth" he replied. "Did it really happen?" Beth asked, looking at the ring on her finger. Danny smiled, "Yes, my love, it did!" He kissed her and then they left.

CHAPTER 10

B eth and Danny were oblivious to the onlookers as he kissed her once more. Walking back to the hotel, they stared into each other's eyes until Beth tripped over something on the path and she fell into his arms for the third time.

"Hey!" said Danny. "You did that on purpose!" as they both laughed.

"Third times the charm!" she replied.

It was like the first time they had been courting. It was easy and they were very happy. They forgot which way they were going and stopped in front of a most beautiful building. They went inside and were amazed at what they saw. It was all stained glass and marble. The red walls and the sunlight streaming through the stained glass made them feel as if they really were in heaven.

"Cough! Cough!" they heard from behind them.

"Oh, we are sorry, we just happened to wander into this exhibit. We will leave now," Danny said.

"No, don't leave, what do you think of this place?" the man inquired.

"Well, it is very beautiful. What is this place called?" Beth asked.

"It is the Tiffany Chapel," he replied and then continued, "I created it so that people could worship art. The stained-glass windows and the marble; these are my creation. I am Louis Comfort Tiffany. My father owns the stained-glass exhibit, and he allowed me to create this marvel on this piece of property."

"Pleased to meet you Mr. Tiffany, I am Danny O'Donnell, and this is Miss Beth Sweeney..."

"Soon to become Mrs. Danny O'Donnell!" Beth said with an enormous smile on her face and showed him the ring.

"That is beautiful, and I am glad that you are here then admiring my chapel."

Beth, who was simply taken with the place, then asked Mr. Tiffany, "Is it going to be used for anything other than an exhibit here?"

Danny looked at Beth, wondering what she was thinking, and Mr. Tiffany wondered the same thing.

"This is such a beautiful chapel, Danny, could we get married here?"

Mr. Tiffany was intrigued. Danny stood there thinking about it, then he said to Beth, "I don't think that he has built this chapel for that but..."

Mr. Tiffany interrupted and said, "Mr. O'Donnell, that is a wonderful idea! What were your plans for a marriage ceremony? Did you have any?"

"We thought we would go home to get married, but we also have been trying to get married for the last 4 years and it seems every time we try something gets in the way. It has been put off for some time now. Even our engagement has been sort of off and on depending on circumstances out of our control."

"Well, when I created this beautiful chapel, I really didn't think about using it for such a purpose, but that would be a wonderful idea since many people seem to be using this venue, the fair, as a place to propose to their loved ones. Perhaps it would be a wonderful idea to gain more attention for this chapel! What do you say? Would you like to get married here? We can set it up by Saturday and you can be married then. I think the afternoon shadows and light, and the electric light streaming in would make a great backdrop for a wedding ceremony," Mr. Tiffany continued.

Danny looked at Mr. Tiffany and thought, 'This would be a great beginning, in fact, we would not be putting it off anymore!' Beth thought about it as well and then said, "We can let everyone know at home that we will have a celebration when we get back home! We already have several friends here with us, so we aren't having a wedding without someone we already know!" Danny agreed with her, and they both said yes. Mr. Tiffany took their names and the hotel they were in and said that it would take a few days before everything was ready.

When Beth and Danny arrived at the hotel room, they both went inside to tell the ladies what happened. Edna and Edith were thrilled and wanted to do whatever they could for them. When they told the Blaine's, Mr. Blaine asked if he could walk Beth down the aisle and Mrs. Blaine asked if she could be her maid of honor. Danny was so happy that he almost forgot to send the telegram. He went downstairs to do that and realized that he needed at least one of his brothers with him to be his best man. So, he also asked if Patrick or Aiden could come to be his best man.

"Oh, Edna, I'm so glad that we are getting to do this! We have waited oh, so long!" Beth said as she was changing her clothes Mrs. Blaine came in just then and asked Beth if she had a wedding dress.

"I have a nice dress for evening but no, I do not have a wedding dress."

"Well, then, we shall get you a wedding dress. I know someone here in Chicago that has a few dresses that we can choose from and fancy them up for a wedding gown. That will be my gift to you!"

Beth was overwhelmed and started to cry. The ladies also had something they were going to give to Beth. They had been planning all along for Beth and Danny's wedding.

Danny sent the telegram and also asked for the family heirloom broach to be sent so Beth could wear it for the wedding. A few hours later, he received confirmation and a telegram that said Aiden would be coming and he would bring the broach as well.

Mr. Blaine knocked on Danny's hotel door and when Danny opened it, he said, "Mr. O'Donnell, do you have a suit that is proper for a wedding?"

"I have only one suit sir and that is all. I use it for special occasions as you know. Why do you ask?"

"Mr. O'Donnell, I am sorry but that will not do. You will come with me. We are going to a men's tailor shop and dress you properly!" Danny looked at him with an embarrassed smile and was about to say, 'no thank you,' when Mr. Blaine used his authority and compelled Danny to go with him.

Beth was so exhausted when she got back. She had the dress, the shoes, the purse, and all the accoutrements that go with a wedding dress. She also had a traveling outfit that Mrs. Blaine provided for her from her own private wardrobe. When the Blaine's had finished with Danny and Beth, they had all the proper accessories and clothing needed for a wedding in a chapel at the World's Fair!

Chapter 11

Aiden got off the train in St Paul and waited for the train to Chicago. He was only carrying one suitcase and wasn't expecting to take much back but hoping to travel the same day as Beth and Danny. Everyone wrote well wishes in the remembrance book that Nancy made. She was now getting a little larger and Dr. Lynne told her to stay off her feet. So, she had Sierra gather the supplies to make a book for Beth.

Patrick made sure that the family heirloom broach was placed in Aiden's suitcase. He was to give it to Beth before she got married. James was very happy and sent along something as well, a bottle of his best Champagne. Patrick was overjoyed but a little unhappy because he had given all the brides away except the one that really mattered to him and his brothers. He didn't add anything to the gifts that everyone else was giving, but his gift would not fit in a suitcase. He and his crew were going to fix up his parent's cabin, adding some bedrooms to accommodate Sierra and Michael later, as well as the hope for children Beth and Danny would have in the future.

While fixing the cabin, Patrick also kept the fireplace intact and had Rusty create a little sitting room for them along with their bedroom and a baby's room. So, when he was not running the camp, he was fixing the original cabin that his parents had lived in. His loggers also built a stable and a barn. The brides that were still nearby made curtains for the windows and helped to provide dishes and other necessities Beth and Danny would need to start a home of their own. This was going to be a big surprise for them, and Aiden was sworn to secrecy.

Beth and Danny were also in a whirlwind of things that had to be done. Mr. Tiffany procured the photographers and decorations for the wedding, although the chapel didn't really need anything extra, but a few ribbons and specially placed decorations enhanced the space, rather than draw attention away from the happy couple.

Late that afternoon, they were all standing in the chapel when the sun was going down. They had just finished deciding that the wedding would be in the afternoon when the electric lights came on and what happened then was nothing short of a miracle. The electric lights streaming through the stained-glass windows gave off a soft glow. The rays of light that came down were in just the right spots. Both Danny and Beth decided they wanted their wedding to be at sundown, just as the sun goes down and the electric lights came on.

Mr. Tiffany agreed. He stated that while it may not be conventional, it would be beautiful. The photographers didn't really like it because their cameras couldn't pick up the light well, but they would try.

"Well, Mr. O'Donnell, you and your lovely lady will have a wonderful wedding!" Mr. Tiffany said to them that evening. "Now I suggest you both go back to the hotel because tomorrow will be a big day for both of you!"

"Thank you, Mr. Tiffany!" Danny said

"Thank you, Mr. Tiffany!" Beth added.

Danny and Beth went back to the hotel and were surprised when they saw Aiden was there. Beth was even more surprised when she saw her sister.

"Sierra!" Beth said as she ran to hug her sister. She missed her sister and brother very much. When Beth and Sierra were finished hugging, Beth looked at Aiden and said, "Thank you, Aiden, I am so glad you brought Sierra!"

"You are welcome, Beth."

"Beth, I asked Aunt Josie and Nancy if I could go. Someone from your family has to be here too!" Sierra said.

"You are right. If I have Aiden, Beth should have Sierra!"

They all laughed and hugged.

"Well, let's get upstairs and we can talk. Danny, Aiden see you tomorrow," Beth said as she guided Sierra to the stairs and up to their hotel room with Edna and Edith.

"Danny, it's so good to see you!" said Aiden.

"It's good to see you as well. Thank you for coming!" Danny helped Aiden bring up the rest of their things. They ended up leaving some things in Danny's room and going to the fair to talk and have a beer.

Aiden was really impressed with the fair. The lights were wonderful, and Danny got caught up on things and what was happening back at home. He explained to Aiden about what Mr. Blaine was planning, as well as what the option was for them. Aiden explained to Danny that they were thinking of opening an office in Olympia to run a crew out there in Yelm and Tenino. They talked long into the night, then fell asleep just about dawn. Unfortunately for Danny, it was a bad idea because he had to get up early to get ready for the wedding.

The wedding day arrived, and a luncheon was provided courtesy of the hotel. Aiden and Sierra were introduced to the Blaine's and Mr. Tiffany, and after lunch the afternoon became very busy. Everyone was rushing around getting everything ready for the wedding ceremony. Mr. Tiffany had the photographers' taking photographs and the newspaper people were writing about the wedding festivities as well.

It was 4:00 pm and everyone was arriving at the chapel for the ceremony. The Justice of the Peace, who was also a minister of the First Presbyterian church, was waiting. Beth and her bridesmaids were at one end of the hall, and Danny and Aiden were at the other. There were many guests that neither Danny nor Beth knew. Although Mrs. Blaine said she would be Beth's Maid of Honor, she provided a dress for Sierra, so Sierra was able to be the Maid of Honor.

The music was about to start, and everyone was in their places. Mr. Blaine was ready to walk Beth down the aisle and Sierra had the flowers to toss. Miss Edna, Miss Edith, and then Mrs. Blaine walked down the aisle. Then the wedding march started and soon, Beth, who was shaking like a tree on Tacobet in the middle of a windstorm, walked down the aisle with Mr. Blaine toward Danny. Danny stood there shaking just as much as Beth. They were both dressed well and when Danny saw Beth coming down the aisle, he took a deep breath and smiled.

Mr. Blaine and Beth reached the front and Danny carefully took Beth's hand and lead her upstairs. Aiden was there to Danny's right, and Sierra was on Beth's left. They stood in front of the minister and solemnly professed their vows. The evening sun shined on them in a display of colored light and as the sunlight drew to a close, the electric lights came on and offered even more exquisite colors, a rainbow effect that was deeper than that of the waning sunlight.

Chapter 12

The wedding had been publicized, and Beth and Danny sat in the carriage waving at all the well-wishers. They were afraid to speak. They were both so overwhelmed because it seemed like they were in a dream. They both looked at each other remembering all the times they came close but never thought they would have made it this far.

After the ride through the fair was done and they were deposited at their hotel, Mr. and Mrs. Blaine met with Danny and Beth. Instead of taking them to Danny's room, the Blaine's escorted them to the bridal suite in the hotel. Mrs. Blaine insisted they spend the next few days together before they left for home as a honeymoon. No one would disturb them, not even Beth's sister. The ladies would see to that!

"I brought all your things Beth, and Aiden deposited your things as well Danny. He will be staying in your room, Danny, for the next couple of days. Edna and Edith send their love and said don't worry about Sierra, they will take care of her as well."

"Thank you" they both said.

Mrs. Blaine kissed Beth on the cheek and told her to call her if she needed anything. Mrs. Blaine sat with Beth the night before explaining things that she may not have known about the first night with her husband. Beth was polite, but she had already heard about it from most of her friends, especially Nancy!

There they stood, both looking at each other knowing, but not knowing, what to say or do next. Beth, being the pragmatic said, "Well, I think we ought to get ready for bed, don't you?"

Danny nodded. He was still processing the fact that he and Beth were finally married. They had waited a long time and he watched as Beth went behind the screen to change her clothes. Mrs. Blaine had placed her night clothes on the chair. These were not her regular night clothes, as they were a bit more revealing. She was surprised and made a little sound.

"Is anything wrong Beth?"

"Oh, no, but don't you have something to slip into for bed?" she said poking her face around the corner of the screen. He looked at her and almost fell over his own feet as he stopped himself from rushing over to hold her closer to him.

"Ah, yes, I guess I do, but I will use the washroom first," he said as he went to the washroom to clean up.

Sunday morning dawned and Danny and Beth were still asleep. Sierra had her breakfast and went to church with the sisters. They decided that after church they would take her to see the fair and the Children's Building. Sierra was 12 and mostly responsible, but on this Sunday, since Beth was not around, she just wanted to go explore. She slowly but deviously slipped out of sight of the ladies. Aiden wasn't walking with them today. He sent a telegram to let everyone in Yelm know that Danny and Beth were now safely married, and no one could stop them from being together forever.

Sierra wound her way around the fairgrounds and soon came upon an old mansion with stores, shops, and apartments. She saw a man standing at the pharmacy counter and went in to see if she could get a soda. Another boy followed her in as well looking for a soda.

"Hello!" Sierra said to the boy. He was a little older than her and she thought he was the cutest thing she ever saw.

"Hello, my name is Frederic, but everyone calls me Freddy." He reached his hand out to shake hers.

"My name is Sierra."

"I can tell you aren't from here!" he said as he accepted the sodas and sat next to her at the counter.

"How can you tell?"

"I can tell because if you were from around here, you wouldn't be coming to this particular pharmacy and having a soda."

"Is there a reason I shouldn't come here? And if so, how come you are here?" Sierra asked defiantly.

"I live here, and I know the rumors. I also know the people here as well!" he said taking another sip of his soda.

"What are these rumors? Are you trying to scare me away?" she said a bit nervously hoping it wasn't more than just a passing chill she was feeling.

Freddy looked at her. He knew that tourists liked stuff like mysteries, so he said, "Well, Sierra, the police have been looking into some disappearances of people who have come to stay at this hotel for the fair. The tourists seem to be disappearing as fast as they show up!" Just then they heard a muffled scream, and both looked at each other. Freddy, who knew the stories, was just as surprised as Sierra.

"Well, did you plan that thinking I would be scared?"

Freddy looked at her and shook his head no. "That is one of the sounds people say they hear in the middle of the night!" he said to Sierra, sipping his soda a little more quickly than before.

"It's not the middle of the night, Freddy. Why did someone scream?"

CHAPTER 13

Edna and Edith were very upset when they found Aiden. They told him that somehow Sierra had disappeared, and they weren't sure where she had gone. Danny and Beth were finally up when they heard what happened and Beth was very upset.

"How can we find her? What if she wandered off somewhere and got lost? What if she's hurt or something? She is only a child!" Beth exclaimed.

"We have got to go find her. Where did you ladies see her last?" Danny asked.

Edna was about to answer when a police officer came in let them know that Sierra had been seen by someone who was leaving the fair. "Sir, are you any relation to a girl named Sierra Sweeney?" the police officer asked Danny.

"Do you know where she is? Can we go pick her up?" Beth answered immediately.

"Ma'am I think it best that you wait here, and we will have a policeman pick her up."

"I would like to come along with you Sir. Danny, you stay with Beth, and we will return soon!" Aiden said.

"But where is she?" Beth asked.

"Beth, I will let you know when we get back!" Aiden replied.

"Well, I am going with you. She is my sister, and I am responsible for her!" Beth was about to push passed the police officer when Danny said, "Beth! You can't go! This isn't like in Yelm. If the police tell you to stay, you have to stay!" Danny took Beth's hand and led her up the stairs. She tried to get away, but Danny stood there pleading with his eyes for her to go with him to their suite.

"Please Beth, let Aiden go. She will be all right!" Beth looked at Danny, and then at Aiden who nodded that all would be well. She had learned to trust the O'Donnell brothers and realized this was not the time nor the place to argue and she went up the stairs with Danny.

Aiden left with the police officer, and they made their way to where Sierra was. The police officer was explaining about the disappearances of local people and tourists, and they were investigating the person who owned the building that the soda shop/pharmacy was located in. Aiden had already heard about it and had stayed clear of the place. Since Sierra was in the soda shop, he would go in to get her. The officer who was watching pointed her out at the counter talking to a boy.

"Sierra, we have to go!" Aiden said quietly. Sierra slid out of her seat and said goodbye to Freddy and left with Aiden. Meanwhile, Freddy shrugged his shoulders, finished his soda, and left to find his friends in the alley.

While they were walking back to their hotel, Aiden said to Sierra, "We were worried about you. The ladies were upset, Danny and Beth took them back to the hotel and are with them. I came looking for you!" Sierra walked alongside Aiden and didn't say anything. She knew she was in trouble, but all she could think about was Freddy. He seemed like such a nice boy, and she wished she could stay a little longer to get to know him.

CHAPTER 14

When they got back to the hotel, Beth was upset and so was Danny. Sierra felt like Danny was more upset with her than anything else.

"So, Sierra what were you thinking leaving the ladies by themselves? You were supposed to accompany them. They took you to the Children's Museum and spent half their day doing things they thought you would like. What do you have to say for yourself?"

Sierra stood there, and Beth was nearby. Since Beth and Danny were married now, it seemed to Sierra like Danny felt he was in charge of her. She didn't like that. She looked at Danny and instead of saying something that wasn't nice, she walked to her room and shut the door. Danny and Beth looked at each other. They were just married and neither of them had any idea what to do.

"Beth, I hope I wasn't too harsh with her, but something could have happened to her," Danny said.

"I know how you feel, I'm glad she is okay, but maybe if I talk to her later when she has calmed down it will be better." Beth was just as perplexed as Danny. They sat up for a while with Edna and Edith discussing the packing, they would be doing tomorrow for their trip back home to Yelm.

Sierra was in her room pouting and she thought to herself, 'I don't want to go home! Not yet anyway. Danny is trying to act like a father to me and I don't need a father!' Then she had an idea. She was going to go find out what the muffled scream was at that other hotel. Freddy said tourists were disappearing and maybe if she did some investigating, she could help the police. She made plans to sneak out later that night when everyone was asleep. She prepared her bed, making sure that it looked like she was sleeping. She heard footsteps coming, so she hid in the closet. Beth peeked in and saw the room was dark. She thought Sierra was in bed, so she closed the door and left. Sierra stepped out of the closet and decided to leave while everyone was sleeping.

She had just gotten to the door of the hotel when Aiden saw her. He followed her out the door, keeping his distance and watching her. Because he was a big brother to Danny, he knew that sometimes kids would do things when they were mad. He did it when he was her age. They all have moments of open defiance. He noticed that she was headed to the old hotel. He had heard the stories about that place, and he knew she would be interested in finding out why. He watched as she searched for a way to get into the hotel. She saw Freddy and was about to run to him to find out what he was doing, when Aiden caught up with her, shushed her, and told her to come with him.

When they were out of earshot and eyeshot, he said to her, "Sierra, this is too dangerous for you!"

"No its not! I can take care of myself!"

Aiden knelt down next to her and continued, "Sierra, the police are investigating real deaths, and real disappearances. They think your friend Freddy may be involved in luring people to this hotel. There is a man who owns this place, a Mr. Holmes. It seems as if they have their eye on him as well. There is real danger here Sierra!" Aiden's face had the look of concern and real fear for her safety.

"What do you mean? Freddy just said that it is to scare tourist." Aiden looked at her, smiled and thought, 'Yes, she is innocent, and it's his job as an uncle to help keep her innocent, but never to lie to her.'

"All right Sierra, you are right, he may be doing this as a tourist attraction to scare tourists, but according to the fair security guards there have been fair goers who have come up missing, not to mention some locals as well. We need to get back to our hotel to be safe." Aiden explained as calmly as he could. He knew more than most because he had stopped in at one of the local saloons and heard the locals talk about what was going on. He himself had almost been roped into checking out the hotel. But he didn't tell Sierra that.

"Aiden, why does Danny think he has to take care of me?" Sierra asked as they walked back to the hotel.

"Well Sierra, Danny feels that since Beth has responsibility for you, he has that responsibility as well now that they are married. His decisions will usually be for the good of all of you!"

"Michael too?" asked Sierra.

"Yes, Michael too." Then Aiden picked her up and carried her quickly back to the hotel. Someone had been following them and he wanted to get her back safely.

The next morning after a breakfast of eggs, bacon, and pancakes (Aunt Jemima), they were all packed and ready to leave. Beth and Sierra were standing by their baggage as Danny and Aiden were helping the ladies with their luggage. Sierra saw Freddy and wanted to go say hi to him, but Beth restrained her.

"Sierra, you are getting old enough now that running off to say hello to a stranger is improper. As you get older, you will need to remember that." Beth said to her quietly.

Sierra looked at Beth and instinctively knew she was right. But she had also seen Beth run after someone if it was a friend of hers. She dismissed that thought as Beth asked her a question, "Sierra, I wanted to ask you about yesterday. I would like to know why you took off and left the ladies to worry about you?"

"I guess I was bored and wanted to find some adventure."

"I realize finding adventure is kind of fun, and I remember when you and Michael took off before, but being 12, Sierra that is a whole new world, and you need to know that you don't need to seek adventure, it comes in many forms. Just like me and Danny, we didn't seek adventure, but adventure found us even when we got married."

Sierra agreed it certainly did find Beth and Danny! "Beth, does growing up mean that I won't ever get to have any fun anymore?"

Beth looked at Sierra and was ready to respond when Danny came up to them and said they were ready to board the train. She told Danny just a moment, and after collecting her thoughts, she said, "No Sierra it doesn't. It just means that there are all kinds of adventures, and they change as you get older."

Sierra looked at her sister and nodded because she knew she was right. It does change as you get older. She remembered Freddy and she wondered if she would ever see him again as they boarded the train and headed back to Yelm.

CHAPTER 15

Patrick picked up the newlyweds from Tacoma and took them to the hotel room they were staying in overnight. The next morning, they left after a quick breakfast and headed home to Yelm.

In Yelm, Josie had everything prepared for the wedding party. The food and decorations were set, and when they arrived, they would be pleasantly surprised. She went up to the balcony to see if she could see them coming. She saw the wagon and rang the bell. Sean was already in port and was waiting as well as the rest of the town. No one had worked that day because the town council had declared a holiday. Even James wasn't in his office. He was dressed in his special blue suit and was ready to congratulate the happy couple.

Nancy had come early, since Dr. Lynne had insisted, she stay seated the whole time. When Patrick arrived, everyone was there to greet them. The happy festive atmosphere was wonderful. The town cheered as Danny got out of the wagon and then helped Beth down. Her grandfather and the boys' uncle were there also to greet them. Their uncle gave her the family heirloom broach, which hadn't gotten to her before they married. Beth's grandfather kissed her and insisted on having the first dance at the party that night.

Beth smiled and said thank you, then Danny whisked her away so they could freshen up for the party. When they returned, the party began. James asked about the champagne and both Danny and Beth blushed and said it was good. They didn't tell him that one glass each was quite sufficient, in fact, they fell asleep in each other's arms and didn't drink the rest of it.

Finally, the party was winding down and it was the Patrick's, the loggers, and James' turn to present Beth and Danny with a most special gift. Patrick brought the wagon around and Rusty took over as Patrick maneuvered Danny and Beth onto the back of the wagon.

"Danny," Beth said, "Where are they taking us?"

Danny said he didn't know but he was sure it wasn't a bad place. They traveled up the mountain and passed by some familiar trees and landmarks. Beth had forgotten the scenery and was confused about where she was. Danny started to get a smile on his face because he remembered the way. The wagon stopped and Patrick got down.

The loggers, millers, ranchers, and other town folks welcomed them as Patrick exclaimed, "Mr. and Mrs. Danny O'Donnell, may I present to you, your new home!"

Beth looked at Danny as he smiled at her. "Did you know about this?" she asked.

"Not until they started up a certain road, then I sort of guessed, but look at the cabin! It is bigger and more wonderful than ever before!"

"That is right Danny, I wanted to give you a gift that would last. We remodeled the cabin a bit. Go inside and take a look." Patrick said.

They went inside and the living area was larger than it had been when Beth and Patrick were there when she was lost. There was a kitchen and a back porch to the right. On the left was a doorway that led to a room with two chairs and a fireplace. Beth went over to the fireplace and looked at it. It was the original fireplace with Patrick's, Aiden's, and Danny's age marks! She made a little cry of joy and tears started to stream down her face.

Danny on the other hand had looked toward the back behind the kitchen, there were two bedrooms and a washroom. They were for Sierra and Michael. He came back and saw Beth in the doorway with tears. He went to her and took his handkerchief to wipe her tears and kissed her gently. They went back into the 'sitting room' and saw the washroom, bedroom, and a small alcove off the bedroom with the cradle. Aiden had made it for them and now Danny was almost in tears as well.

"Danny, I hope you enjoy your new home," Patrick said, "We will leave you to get settled. Everything is here that you need. Go ahead and get to know your new home and each other. Sierra and Michael are staying in town and will join you in a week."

Danny smiled and shook Patrick's hand. Beth gave him a kiss on the cheek. Then they heard a loud 'MOOOO!' and a couple of whinnies.

"That is Bessy, the cow, and of course your horses out in the barn and stable. Bessy needs attention soon, so one of you will have to milk her. She has a baby we haven't named yet!" Michael said. Beth hadn't seen her little brother throughout the whole party and went over to hug him and thank him. Michael hugged her, then they all said goodbye and left the happy couple. The whole group cheered and shouted until they were close to town, and suddenly there was silence.

Beth and Danny looked at each other and then without a word, Danny took his bride and carried her into their bedroom and...well, you know the rest of the story!